Published by The Last Pharaoh Publishing
ISBN: 979-8-218-61250-4
First Edition.
This is a work of fiction. Any resemblance to actual persons, living or dead,
or actual events is purely coincidental.
Cover design by J. Reyes

The Spark of Curiosity

The street was quiet, save for the soft hum of flickering streetlights overhead. Caleb's sneakers scuffed against the cracked pavement as he walked, his hands stuffed deep into the pockets of his worn hoodie. He didn't have a destination—he rarely did. Nights like these, the streets felt like home. The empty sidewalks, the faint glow of distant headlights, and the occasional muffled laughter from open windows all seemed to wrap him in an invisible cocoon.

It was better than the group home, where the air was heavy with stale complaints and the constant drone of the television. Here, at least, Caleb could think.

As he turned a corner, a flickering light caught his eye. The storefront window of an electronics shop stood out like a beacon, a dozen TVs playing the same video in synchronized clarity. Caleb slowed his pace, his gaze drawn to the largest screen in the center.

On the screen, a man sat cross-legged on a grassy hill, his hands forming a triangle over his stomach. His eyes were closed, and his face was serene, as if he were somewhere far beyond the troubles of the world.

Caleb tilted his head, intrigued. The video's narrator spoke in a soothing tone: "Meditation is the key to unlocking the mind's hidden potential. The ancients believed that energy flows from the earth to the body, creating a harmony that transcends the physical plane."

The camera panned to a group of people meditating together under a starry sky, their breathing synchronized, their faces calm. Caleb's stomach twisted—not with hunger, but with something deeper. Longing.

"Unlocking the mind's hidden potential...?" he muttered under his breath. The idea sounded ridiculous, but for some reason, he couldn't look away.

The video continued: "Close your eyes. Focus on your breathing. Let your mind clear, and feel the energy of the universe flow through you."

Caleb took a step closer to the glass. For a moment, he imagined himself sitting on that grassy hill, away from the city's noise and his own restless thoughts. The idea of clearing his mind, of finding peace—even if just for a moment—seemed... impossible. And yet, it was tempting.

He glanced around the empty street, then back at the screen. "Energy flowing through the body... harmony..." The words echoed in his head as he continued down the sidewalk, his pace slower now, his mind buzzing with the possibility.

When he finally reached the group home, Caleb slipped into his shared room, careful not to wake anyone. He sat cross-legged on the floor, mimicking the man in the video. His hands trembled slightly as he formed the triangle over his stomach.

The room was dim, the faint glow of a streetlamp outside casting long shadows on the walls. Caleb closed his eyes, his breathing shallow at first, then gradually slowing. For the first time in years, the noise in his head began to quiet.
And then he felt it.

The Awakening of the Serpent

The night was still. Caleb's breath deepened, his mind settling into an eerie silence he hadn't known before. The noise of the world faded—the murmurs of distant traffic, the occasional creak of the old group home, even the soft rustle of his own clothing as he sat motionless.

And then... it began.

A sudden chill swept through the air, curling around his skin like unseen fingers. Caleb's eyelids fluttered, but he kept them shut, the warmth of his own breath steady against his lips.

Then he felt it.

A whisper of movement, so faint he almost mistook it for a trick of his imagination. But it grew stronger. A slithering, smooth, coiling weight curling around his ankle. His breath hitched.

The sensation became too real, too vivid.

Something was crawling across his feet.

His body stiffened as his mind screamed at him to move, to run, but he was paralyzed—trapped in a trance deeper than anything he had ever known.

And then, the weight increased.

A massive serpent.

Not just any snake—but something ancient, primal, beyond comprehension.

He didn't need to open his eyes to see it. It wanted him to know it was there.

It coiled up his leg, its scales like molten metal—a living river of scarlet, shimmering under an unseen light. Each scale pulsed with a deep glow, as though it held the very essence of embers within.

Its weight pressed down on his body, not crushing him, but claiming him.

Then—the eyes.

Caleb didn't know how he saw them with his eyes closed, but there they were. Two orbs of fire, burning like twin suns, radiating power older than time itself.

A voice, or maybe a whisper that wasn't spoken aloud but felt, slithered into his mind:

"You are mine."

And then it struck.

The serpent plunged into his foot.

A piercing heat—like liquid fire—shot through him as if the creature had not just touched him but become him. His veins burned, his bones trembled, and something seared into his sole, branding him in a way that could never be undone.

His mouth opened in a silent scream, but no sound escaped.

He was locked inside this moment, trapped between terror and something else—something darker, deeper, inevitable.

Then, in a single heartbeat, the vision shattered.

Caleb gasped, his lungs clawing for air as his body jerked backward, his back slamming into the wooden floor of the group home. His limbs convulsed as if the last remnants of the serpent were still inside him, coiling around his bones, squeezing his breath.

And then, it was gone.

Silence.

But his foot burned.

Drenched in sweat, his shaking hands reached down, fingers trembling as they brushed against the sole of his foot. His breath hitched.

There was a mark.

Small. Unmistakable.

His stomach lurched. It wasn't a cut, not a bruise—but something ancient, something unnatural.

And Caleb knew, in that instant, that whatever had just happened wasn't a dream.

Something had awakened.

And it would never let him go.

The Awakening of the Mark

Caleb lay on the wooden floor, his chest rising and falling in uneven gasps. His skin felt damp with sweat, but the heat wasn't fading—it was inside him, coursing through his veins like a living current. His foot still tingled, but now it wasn't from pain.

It was glowing.

A soft, pulsating light shone from the sole of his foot, casting a faint golden-red hue on the floorboards beneath him. His breath caught in his throat as he stared in disbelief.

"What the hell..." he whispered, dragging himself upright.

His fingers trembled as they brushed against the mark. The moment he touched it, a strange sensation rippled through his body—like static electricity, but deeper. It wasn't just on his skin. It was inside him.

Then, the world changed.

First, his hearing.

A wave of noise slammed into his eardrums, and he clamped his hands over his ears, wincing. It was too much—too loud. The distant drip of a leaking faucet, the creaking of wood under shifting weight in the next room, the low murmur of someone whispering in their sleep down the hall.

Even outside... he could hear the city breathing.

The rumble of car engines, the rustling of wind through trees, the subtle, rhythmic tapping of a raccoon's claws against pavement. Every sound, every vibration, every shift in the world—he could hear it all.

His heart pounded. "What the hell is happening to me?"

Then, his reflexes.

Caleb pushed himself off the floor, but the moment he moved—his body reacted faster than his mind.

A cockroach scurried across the floor, and before he even thought about it, his hand lashed out like a whip, Snap.
His fingers clamped around it in midair.

His stomach churned in disgust, and he immediately let go, watching the insect drop to the floor and scurry away. His hands shook, but not from fear—from the sheer shock of his own speed.

That wasn't normal. That wasn't human.
His breathing quickened, his senses overwhelmed, but it wasn't over.

Then, his vision.

The dimly lit room brightened—not from the streetlamp outside, but from his own eyes adjusting.

Everything sharpened. The darkness peeled away, replaced by a world of ultraviolet hues and glowing outlines. He could see details in the shadows that had been invisible before—dust particles floating in the air, faint scratches on the wooden doorframe, tiny veins in the leaves of a dying potted plant by the window.

He turned toward the window, eyes widening.

Outside, the night was alive.

Neon signs no longer glowed in just red and blue—they shimmered in colors he had never seen before. The faintest movements became sharp and precise—he could see a moth's wings fluttering in slow motion as it danced around a distant light.

And in the alleyway beyond...

A cat hunting a rat, both creatures moving in what should have been darkness, but to Caleb, they were outlined in pure clarity. He saw the cat's muscles tense before it pounced.

His breath hitched.

He could see in the dark.

The realization hit him like a freight train. This wasn't just one thing—his entire body was changing. His senses, his speed, his vision—it was like he had been reprogrammed.

All because of the mark.

His heart pounded against his ribs. He wasn't scared—he was in awe.

His fingers brushed over the glowing imprint on his foot again, feeling its warmth.

He didn't know what was happening.

He didn't know why it was happening.

But one thing was certain.

He wasn't the same anymore.

The Escape into the Night

Caleb's chest tightened as the reality of what had just happened sank in. His senses were still on fire, every sound, every flicker of movement too sharp, too clear. The mark on his foot pulsed softly, like a living ember embedded in his skin.

This isn't normal. This isn't possible.

Panic clawed at his throat. He couldn't stay here.

They'd notice.

The other kids in the group home—the caretakers—someone would see the glow, would see that he wasn't the same anymore.

His breathing shallow, Caleb grabbed his worn-out sneakers and quickly shoved them on, hiding the mark beneath the fabric. His hands trembled as he laced them up, as if tying the shoes could somehow hold his world together.

I have to get out of here.

Moving fast—too fast—he threw on his hoodie, shoving his hands deep into the pockets, trying to suppress the rising wave of fear pressing against his ribs. His legs felt restless, wired, like they were too light—as if running would be easier than walking.

The floor creaked beneath his weight as he stepped toward the door, and suddenly—

He heard breathing.

His head snapped toward the bunk beds. Someone shifted in their sleep, a quiet, almost imperceptible exhale—but to Caleb, it was loud. His newfound hearing picked up every detail—the way their blankets rustled, the subtle shift in their heartbeat.

He clenched his jaw. Too much. It was too much.

Slowly, carefully, he turned the knob, willing the old door not to groan under his touch. He slipped out into the dimly lit hallway, his steps silent, precise—like an instinct buried deep in him had awakened.

As he passed the office, the flickering glow of a small TV played across the walls. The overnight caretaker sat slumped in his chair, barely awake, his fingers absently flipping through a magazine. The glow from the emergency exit sign cast a dull red light over the floor.

Almost there.

Caleb's heart pounded as he reached the front door. His fingers gripped the handle, and he pushed.

The door groaned.

The caretaker stirred.

Caleb's pulse spiked, every nerve in his body going into overdrive. If he turned—if he made eye contact—he'd be caught. He knew it.

The man shifted in his chair... then let out a slow snore.

Caleb exhaled in relief.

And then he ran.

The Streets: The Night Feels Different

The cold air hit him like a shock as he stepped onto the street. The city stretched before him, but something about it felt new, altered.

The streetlights flickered overhead, their glow casting elongated shadows—but Caleb could see past them. The darkness no longer felt suffocating. It felt clear. Defined.

His feet hit the pavement, but he barely felt the impact—he was moving too smoothly, too effortlessly.

Everything about him had changed.

He didn't know where he was going. He just knew he couldn't stay.

Into the Unknown

Caleb ran.

The city stretched out before him, but he didn't process the streets, the alleys, the neon reflections in puddles on the pavement. His body moved effortlessly, his strides longer, faster, as if his muscles already knew how to glide through the night without effort.

His heart pounded, but not from exhaustion.

I should be tired. I should be out of breath.

But he wasn't.

He kept running. Faster.

A blur of streetlights. Faint voices in the distance. A dog barking three blocks away—he could hear it clear as day. He pushed forward, deeper into the city's quieter veins, moving without a destination.

Then, at last, he saw it.

An abandoned building at the edge of town, swallowed by creeping ivy and broken windows. A rusted "NO TRESPASSING" sign hung loosely on the chain-link fence, swaying in the night breeze. The place had been dead for years, forgotten by the world.

Perfect.

Caleb climbed over the fence with an ease that shouldn't have been possible, his body reacting before his mind even caught up. He landed lightly, barely making a sound as he stepped inside.

The air smelled of dust and decay. Graffiti covered the walls, a mix of old gang tags and half-finished symbols. The moonlight barely reached inside, yet Caleb could see everything.

He swallowed, stepping deeper into the darkness, but the moment he did—

The mark on his foot pulsed.

A single warm throb that rippled through his leg.

He staggered, pressing his hand against the wall. His head felt light, electric. The air buzzed, like the whole world had shifted around him.

Then, his hearing stretched.

Too far.

The city's whispers came crashing down on him all at once. Footsteps miles away. The hum of streetlights. The faint drip, drip of water from a leaking pipe somewhere in the building. His mind couldn't shut it out.

His breathing became shallow.

Too much.

He clenched his fists, pressing his back against the cold wall, squeezing his eyes shut—

But then, a new sound.

Not from the city. Not from the building.

From inside his own mind.

A hiss.

Low. Ancient. Patient.

Caleb's eyes snapped open.

Across the room, where the moonlight barely kissed the floorboards, something moved.

A shadow.

Long. Slithering. Watching.

Caleb's pulse slammed against his ribs.

The snake.

It wasn't over. It was still here. It had followed him.

And then—the eyes.

Burning red-orange, like twin embers, they blinked open in the darkness, locked onto him.

The hissing grew louder. Not from fear.

From recognition.

"You ran... but you are mine."

The voice wasn't spoken. It was inside him.

The air around Caleb tightened, the weight of something immense and unseen pressing down on his chest. The darkness around the snake rippled, as if the very air bent around its presence.

And in that moment, Caleb knew.

This wasn't just an accident.

The mark. The abilities. The awakening.

It had all been planned.

The Voice of the Serpent

Caleb's breath hitched, his body frozen against the wall as the eyes of fire stared into him.

The snake wasn't outside of him.

It was inside.

It had slithered into his bones, his blood, his mind.

And now, it spoke.

Not with a voice carried through the air—but within him, as if it had always been there, waiting for the right moment to wake up.

"You ran... but you are mine."

Caleb's pulse pounded against his ribs. His hands curled into fists. No. This isn't real. This isn't happening.

But then, the mark on his foot throbbed, sending another wave of heat through his veins. A whisper of something old, ancient, powerful curled around his thoughts.

"I chose you."

Caleb squeezed his eyes shut, shaking his head. No. No one chose me. He had spent his whole life being unwanted—shuffled from place to place, never belonging to anyone. Why now? Why this?

But the voice was relentless, smooth as silk, heavy as stone.

"You are the last hope of a long-forgotten lineage."

A chill raced down his spine.

His breathing grew shallow, his chest tight. The words sank into him, weighty and undeniable.

A lineage?

His past was nothing. He was just another kid tossed aside by the system, another nobody.

But now, something older than time itself was telling him that wasn't true.

His fingers dug into the fabric of his hoodie. What does that even mean? What lineage? What hope?

He wanted to reject it. To tell the voice to shut up.

But deep down...

He felt it.

A thread of truth.

Something inside him already knew.

Like a door that had been locked for centuries had just creaked open.

He swallowed hard, forcing his voice out. "What... do you want from me?"

The snake hissed, the sound vibrating inside his skull.

"Not yet."

The fire in its eyes dimmed. The heavy presence coiling around him loosened—not gone, but waiting.

"Soon... you will understand."

And then—silence.

The weight vanished.

The heat cooled.

Caleb gasped, nearly falling forward as his knees threatened to give out. His hands shook as he pressed them against the wall, his body still humming with the remnants of whatever had just happened.

The world around him settled.

The wind outside whistled through shattered windows. A loose door creaked somewhere deep in the abandoned building.

But inside him...

Something had changed forever.

He clenched his fists, staring down at his sneakers, knowing that underneath—the mark was still there.

And now, he had a secret he could never escape.

Denial and Doubt

Caleb sat on the cold concrete floor of the abandoned building, his back pressed against the wall, his legs drawn up toward his chest. The mark on his foot had stopped glowing, but the sensation of it—the weight of it—lingered in his bones.

His fingers curled into fists as he stared at the empty space before him, his mind replaying the events of the past hour like a glitching reel of film.

The meditation. The snake. The mark. The voice.

"You are the last hope of a long-forgotten lineage."

A bitter laugh slipped past his lips. "What the hell does that even mean?"

His own voice sounded foreign to him—like it belonged to someone else. Someone caught between reality and something impossible.

Caleb shook his head, running a hand through his messy hair. Why did I even try this? He had never meditated in his life. He barely even believed in that stuff.

And yet... something had made him stop and listen to that video in the store window. Something had made him sit down, close his eyes, and try.

And now?

Now he had a burning mark on his foot, senses that made the world feel too loud, too clear, too sharp, and a voice in his head whispering that he was part of something he didn't want to be a part of.

His jaw clenched.

No. This isn't real.

He pushed himself up onto his feet, pacing the room. "It's just—just some hallucination. Maybe I didn't sleep enough. Maybe it's all in my head."

But even as he said it, he knew it was a lie.

The mark. The fire in his veins. The way his body moved faster than his own thoughts.

He stopped pacing and pressed his fists against his temples.

I don't want this.

His whole life, he had been alone. Nobody had ever come looking for him, no long-lost family, no secret destiny waiting for him in some hidden temple.

He was just a kid from nowhere.
And yet, the words of the snake wouldn't leave him.

"I chose you."

Caleb gritted his teeth.

No. He refused to be chosen by something he didn't even understand.
Whatever this was—whatever was happening to him—he wanted nothing to do with it.
And he was going to prove it.
If this was just some hallucination, then he should be able to ignore it. He would go back, lay low, and let this thing fade away.
Because if he didn't?
Then he wasn't just running from a voice in his head.
He was running from who he was becoming.

Caleb Tries to Return to Normal

The night air had cooled by the time Caleb reached the edge of the city. His heart had stopped hammering in his chest, but his mind was still spinning, trying to make sense of everything.

He kept his hood up as he walked, head down, hands shoved into his pockets. He needed to think. He needed to get a grip.

This wasn't real.

It couldn't be real.

If he just acted normal, kept his head down, maybe it would all go away. Maybe tomorrow, he'd wake up and the mark would be gone.

His feet carried him back toward the group home. The streetlights buzzed overhead, casting long shadows across the cracked pavement.

And then—

A sharp noise cut through the air.

A dog barking. A trash can tipping over. The quick, panicked footsteps of someone running.

Caleb's head snapped up before he even realized he'd reacted. His ears caught everything.

A guy—maybe a teenager—bolted across the street, clutching something under his jacket. Behind him, an older man—the store owner, probably—yelled, "Hey! Stop, thief!"

Caleb barely processed the scene before something shifted inside him.

It was instinct.

His body moved before his mind caught up.

The kid was fast. But Caleb—

Caleb was faster.

His legs kicked into motion, his strides longer, smoother. The wind rushed past him, but it wasn't resistance—it was effortless. The thief's frantic breathing was loud in Caleb's ears, his heartbeat hammering like a drum.

Caleb closed the distance in seconds.

Too fast.

The moment he realized it—his foot clipped the pavement.

His body lurched forward. He hit the ground, hard—palms scraping against the rough asphalt.

Pain flared. His breath hitched.

But then—

It was gone.

His hands—they should have been torn up. Bleeding.

He glanced down.

Nothing.

The skin was smooth, unbroken.

A cold chill ran up his spine.

His fingers brushed over his palm, his breathing uneven. He'd just—he'd just hit the ground. He felt the scrape. But now...

The thief had vanished, disappearing into the night. The store owner was still yelling, but Caleb barely heard him.

His pulse pounded in his ears as he stared at his unmarked hands.

No cuts. No bruises. Nothing.

His stomach twisted.

No.

No.

He shoved his hands into his hoodie pocket, forcing himself to move—to walk away.

Forget it. It's nothing. I imagined it.

But deep down, he knew.

Something was very, very wrong.

Hiding the Truth

Caleb's steps slowed as he approached the group home, his breath steadying, his hands still shoved deep into his hoodie pockets.

Just act normal.

He climbed the front steps carefully, the old wooden planks creaking softly beneath his weight. The dim porch light flickered above, casting weak, yellow light across the chipped paint of the door.

His fingers hesitated on the doorknob.

For a split second, a whisper of doubt crept into his mind.

What if I can't hide it?

What if the others notice something different about him? The way he moved, the way his senses had sharpened—what if they could see it in his eyes?

A cold shiver ran through him.

But then, he pushed the thought aside.

No one would notice.

Because nothing happened.

That's what he'd tell himself. That's what he had to believe.

With a slow exhale, he turned the knob and slipped inside.

Inside the Group Home

The air inside was stale, filled with the familiar murmurs of sleep, the low hum of a television left on somewhere down the hall. The glow from a single nightlight cast long shadows across the walls.
Everyone was asleep.

Perfect.

Moving silently, Caleb walked down the narrow hallway toward his room. His movements were... too smooth. Too precise.

Like he was more aware of every shift in the floorboards, every flicker of motion in the dark.

He forced himself to ignore it.

When he reached his shared room, he eased the door open and slipped inside. The other guys were already asleep, their steady breathing filling the small space.

He bent down, tugging his sneakers off, careful not to let them make a sound. His pulse hitched when he saw the faint glow beneath his foot.

The mark.

Still there.

Still real.

His stomach twisted.

Quickly, he yanked his blanket over himself, tucking his foot deep beneath the sheets, shielding it from sight—as if covering it could somehow make it disappear.

He lay still, staring at the ceiling.

Nothing happened tonight.

Tomorrow, everything would go back to normal.

That's what he told himself.

That's what he had to believe.

But as his eyes finally drifted shut, deep in the quiet of the night—

He swore he heard the faintest whisper.

A hiss.
Low. Ancient.
Waiting.

The Morning After – Trying to Be Normal

Sunlight streamed through the cracked blinds, casting faint golden lines across the ceiling. Caleb stirred, blinking against the light, his mind groggy but clear.

For a moment, he almost forgot.

Almost.

Then, the memory of last night flooded back—the meditation, the snake, the mark, the impossible speed, the cut that never happened.

His body tensed under the sheets.

Slowly, cautiously, he wiggled his toes. No pain. No stiffness. He shifted his legs, his arms—nothing felt different.

Maybe... maybe it's over.

He exhaled slowly, pushing back the blanket and sitting up. His foot was hidden beneath his sock. Good. He wasn't about to check. He wasn't going to look.

Not today.

Instead, he forced himself to move, to act normal.

The other guys in the room were waking up too. Ethan, his closest thing to a friend in this place, was stretching with a loud yawn from the top bunk.

"Dude, you look like crap," Ethan muttered, rubbing his eyes.

Caleb snorted, pulling his hoodie over his head. "Thanks, man. Always a confidence booster."

Ethan grinned, jumping down from his bunk with a thud. Caleb heard it too clearly—the weight of Ethan's landing, the faint scratch of his socks against the wooden floor.

Too much detail.

Caleb swallowed hard. Ignore it. Be normal.

The other guys were already moving around, getting dressed, joking, messing with each other like always. It was routine. Familiar. Safe.

Caleb tried to sink into it.

Ethan nudged him as they walked out toward breakfast. "You okay, man? You seem kinda... I dunno. Tense."

Caleb forced a shrug. "Didn't sleep great."

Not a lie. Just not the full truth.

"Yeah, you were tossing a lot," Ethan said. "You having those weird dreams again?"

Caleb hesitated. Weird dreams. If only it had just been a dream.

"Something like that." He forced a chuckle, shoving his hands in his pockets. "Maybe I should stop watching creepy videos before bed."

Ethan smirked. "Yeah, no kidding."

Caleb almost relaxed as they reached the dining area. The smell of stale cereal, toast, and burnt eggs filled the air. The same old group home breakfast. Something predictable. Something safe.

Maybe today would be normal.

Maybe if he just kept moving, kept playing along, he could bury last night deep enough that it wouldn't matter.

At least for now.

A Normal Day (For Now)

The rest of the morning passed in familiar routines.

Breakfast was the same as always—cheap cereal, soggy toast, and eggs that tasted like rubber. Caleb sat with Ethan and a few of the other guys, nodding along to their conversation about some dumb action movie they wanted to sneak-watch later.

He laughed at the right moments. He reacted the way he always did. Nothing was different.

That was the goal.

After breakfast, the group home staff went through their usual routine—chores, school prep, reminders about rules nobody actually followed.

Caleb went through the motions. Made his bed. Helped clean up the kitchen. Avoided eye contact with any of the caretakers, just in case they saw something in his face—some sign that he wasn't quite the same anymore.
But no one did.
Because nothing had changed.
At least, that's what he kept telling himself.
Later, he and Ethan killed time in the tiny rec room, flipping through channels on the old TV, talking about nothing important.

For a few blessed hours, Caleb almost forgot.
Almost.
No glowing mark. No strange whispers. No impossible reflexes.
Just a regular kid in a regular place, wasting time with his friends.
It felt good. Safe.
Like maybe, just maybe, last night hadn't changed anything at all.

The Last Normal Day

The rest of the day slipped by like any other.

Lunch was bland. Chores were boring. The afternoon passed in lazy conversations, cheap jokes, and the dull comfort of routine.

For a few fleeting hours, Caleb let himself believe it.

That last night was nothing.
That the mark on his foot was just a weird coincidence.
That the whisper in his head was just a bad dream.

That he was just a normal kid.

Evening: A Quiet Moment

By the time the sun dipped below the horizon, the group home settled into its usual evening rhythm.

Some of the younger kids were messing around, watching cartoons. A few of the older ones—Ethan included—were huddled in the rec room, talking about sneaking out later to meet up with some girls.

Caleb just sat back, listening.

Not speaking much. Just... existing.

Savoring it.

Because deep down, something in his gut told him—

This was the last time.

The last time he would sit here, carefree, surrounded by people who didn't know what he really was.
The last time his biggest problem was sneaking out without getting caught.
The last time he would belong in this world.

A strange, unshakable weight settled over his chest.
He pushed it down.
Shoved his hands in his hoodie pockets. Forced a smirk when Ethan elbowed him about skipping out on the fun.
Everything was fine.
Everything was normal

Night Falls: The Final Quiet

By the time night came, the house had gone still.

The distant hum of a TV. The occasional creak of floorboards. Soft breathing in the dark.

Caleb lay on his bunk, staring at the ceiling.

Waiting.

For what, he didn't know.

But something in the air felt... different.

Like a storm, quiet and unseen, waiting just beyond the horizon.

He pulled his blanket up, tucking his foot out of sight. His muscles ached from trying to ignore everything.

Tomorrow would come.

And with it—

Everything would change.

A Small Slip-Up

The next day felt almost normal.

Caleb moved through the motions—breakfast, chores, and meaningless conversations—pushing down everything that had happened the night before.

Just keep going.
Ignore it.
Pretend it didn't happen.

But no matter how hard he tried to convince himself, something felt off.

His body felt too light, too balanced—like every movement was effortless. His hearing still picked up too much, but he trained himself to tune it out.

Everything was fine.

Until it wasn't.

The Slip-Up: A Moment of Instinct

It happened fast.

The group was outside, messing around in the worn-down basketball court behind the home. The pavement was cracked, the hoop barely hanging onto its rusted pole.

Ethan and a few of the guys were goofing around, throwing half-court shots and failing miserably. Caleb leaned against the fence, half-paying attention, letting the sounds blur together.

Then—

A loud shout.

Something fast, heavy, and solid came flying straight toward his head.

Without thinking—

Caleb moved.

His body twisted before his brain even registered the danger. His arm shot up, fingers snatching the ball out of the air mid-flight—

With one hand.

The impact should've hurt. The force should've knocked him back.

But it didn't.

He had caught it perfectly, his feet planted like he hadn't even moved.

The guys around him froze.

"Whoa," Ethan blinked. "Dude... what was that?"

Caleb felt his stomach drop.

Too fast.
Too natural.
Too obvious.

He forced a casual shrug, tossing the ball back. "Lucky catch."

Ethan frowned, tilting his head. "Nah, man. That was crazy. You didn't even flinch."

The others muttered in agreement, eyes lingering on him just a little too long.

Caleb ignored the knot tightening in his chest. He forced a smirk. "What, you jealous?"

The tension broke as Ethan laughed, shaking his head. "Yeah, yeah, whatever."

The others moved on. The game continued.

But Caleb knew.

For the first time, he had slipped up.

And worse—

Someone had noticed.

The Video Goes Online

Unbeknownst to Caleb, one of the younger kids—Nathan, a 13-year-old who was always glued to his phone—had been recording the basketball game.

Not for any real reason. Just boredom.

But when he played back the footage later that evening, something caught his attention.

Caleb's reaction.

The ball had been coming at him fast, way too fast for a normal reaction. And yet, he caught it perfectly.
Nathan replayed it. Then again.

Slowed it down.
It looked... wrong.
Caleb barely moved. The ball should've hit him before he could react. But somehow, he had moved before impact.
It was almost inhuman.
Nathan squinted, debating if it was just a trick of the camera.
But then—he shrugged.
Either way, it looked cool.

So, without thinking much of it, he uploaded it to a random sports clip account he ran on social media.
Caption: "This dude got Spider-Man reflexes lol"
A few of his followers liked it. Someone commented:
"That reaction time is insane"
"Bro has Ultra Instinct"
Nothing crazy. Just a random video.For now.

The Next Day: Caleb Finds Out

The morning started normal.

Caleb woke up, went through the usual routine, and forced himself to act like yesterday never happened.

At breakfast, Ethan was scrolling on his phone, smirking. "Yo, Caleb. You're famous."

Caleb blinked. "What?"

Ethan turned his phone around.

There it was.

The video.

The clip of him snatching the ball out of midair like it was nothing.

A small post, nothing viral—but more than enough for Caleb's stomach to drop.

Nathan grinned across the table. "That was crazy, dude. Didn't know you had reflexes like that."

Caleb forced a laugh. "Yeah... just lucky, I guess."

Ethan snorted. "Nah, man. That was, like... professional-level timing."

Caleb shrugged it off, pretending it didn't matter.

But deep inside—

He knew this wasn't good.

It wasn't a big deal yet...

But what if someone really looked at it?

What if someone noticed what he was trying to hide?

For the first time, he realized—

He couldn't stay here much longer.

The Video Gains Traction & Caleb Starts Thinking About Leaving

By the afternoon, the video had picked up more views than expected.

Not viral in the millions, but definitely bigger than a throwaway post.

People were sharing it, commenting things like:

"Nah, that's not normal. Slow it down. Bro moved before the ball even got close."

"That's like ESP or some superpower reflex sht."*

"Fake? Looks kinda real though..."

Someone even slowed it down and re-uploaded it, highlighting how Caleb's reaction time didn't make sense.

It wasn't mainstream news or anything, but in the small corners of the internet where people obsessed over unexplained stuff, the video wasn't going unnoticed.

Caleb Notices the Shift

By the time dinner rolled around, Caleb could feel it.

The stares.

Not suspicious, not hostile—but... curious.

Nathan, Ethan, and a few others kept bringing it up, joking about how maybe Caleb had some hidden talent.

Caleb laughed along with them, playing it off.

But inside, his stomach twisted.

This wasn't normal attention.

This wasn't the kind of thing he could ignore.

That Night: Thinking About Leaving

Caleb lay in his bunk, staring at the ceiling, heart pounding.

He had been trying so damn hard to pretend he could stay here. That things could go back to normal.

But now?

Now his face was on the internet. His name wasn't attached, sure—but what if someone recognized him? What if this was just the beginning?

He exhaled, running a hand through his hair.

I can't stay here.

The words felt final.

The group home had never really been a home—but at least it had been stable.

Now?

It was just a place he was trapped in.

And he needed to get out.

Sneaking Out & Finding Comfort in the Abandoned House

That night, after everyone was asleep, Caleb slipped out.

No noise. No hesitation. He had done this before.

The night air was cool, the streets mostly empty, the world quiet except for the occasional rustling leaves and distant sirens.

As he made his way toward the abandoned house, something inside him settled.

This place—the group home—wasn't his future.

He didn't know what was, but this... this was a start.

Inside the Abandoned House

The air was stale, filled with dust and memories long forgotten. But it didn't feel... bad.

It felt isolated. Safe.

Caleb moved through the dark, but his eyes adjusted instantly. Shadows peeled back, revealing every corner of the room in crisp detail.

He had been here before, but now?

Now he needed to make it his.

He checked the second floor, stepping carefully, testing the strength of the floorboards. In one of the back rooms, he found exactly what he was hoping for—

An old mattress.

It was beat-up, covered in a thin layer of dust, but it was something.

Caleb dragged it closer to the window, where the moonlight spilled in, giving the room a dim, silver glow.

He sat down.

Then laid back.

And for the first time in a long time, he felt at peace.

Settling In: The Feeling of Freedom

It wasn't much.

No blankets. No pillow. No real security.

But it was his.

He stared at the ceiling, listening to the distant hum of the city, letting himself sink into the moment.

For the first time, he wasn't just another kid in a system.

For the first time, he had a choice.
He wasn't sure when he would leave the group home for good.
But tonight, as he closed his eyes in the quiet of his own space, he knew—
It wouldn't be long now.
Preparing for His New Life & Testing His Abilities
Over the next few nights, Caleb kept sneaking out.

Each time, he brought something small from the group home. Nothing noticeable.

A blanket. A hoodie. A flashlight. A couple of snacks.

Little by little, the abandoned house became his home.

The old mattress was still rough, but with the blanket draped over it, it was warm enough. He stuffed the hoodie under his head like a pillow—not perfect, but better than nothing.
It wasn't about comfort.
It was about freedom.

Testing His Abilities: The First Real Experiment

One night, after dropping off some extra food, Caleb sat on the floor, staring at his hands.

He knew something had changed in him.

And now that he was finally alone, he could stop pretending.

He stretched out his fingers, flexing them slowly, feeling the subtle hum of energy beneath his skin.

His body felt... lighter. Stronger. Like it was waiting for something.

What else can I do?

Test 1: Strength & Reflexes

He stood up and focused on his movements.

A quick step forward. A turn. A jump.

Fast. Too fast.

He barely even tried, yet his feet barely touched the floor before he was already moving again.

A small, half-hearted punch into the air—too sharp, too precise.

He dropped into a crouch.

Then sprang up.

His body reacted perfectly, like it knew exactly how to move before he even thought about it.

Damn...

A grin flickered across his face.

It felt right.

Like his body was finally working the way it was meant to.

Test 2: Night Vision

He let the flashlight stay off and stood in the darkness.

The moon was barely out. The room was pitch black.

But Caleb?

He could see everything.

The faint cracks in the floorboards. The dust particles floating in the air. The faded graffiti on the farthest wall.

It wasn't just seeing in the dark.

It was more than that.

Colors looked different. Shadows had depth. The world felt alive in ways he had never noticed before.

Test 3: Hearing

Closing his eyes, he focused.

The house was still. Silent.

But the city wasn't.

Far in the distance—a dog barking.

A car alarm three blocks away.

The wind rattling a street sign a mile down the road.

Too much. Too clear.

He exhaled sharply, shaking his head. "Okay... that's insane."

The First Realization: He's Not Normal Anymore

As he sat back down, heart still racing, Caleb finally admitted it.

I'm different.

And there was no going back.

He wasn't just a kid from a group home anymore.

Something inside him had changed forever.

And whatever it was...

It was only getting stronger.

Testing His Speed

The night air was crisp and cool as Caleb slipped through the quiet streets, his hood pulled low over his head.

He had been sneaking out for days now, bringing supplies, testing his abilities in the safety of the abandoned house.

But there was one thing he hadn't tested yet.

His speed.

And tonight, he was going to find out just how fast he really was.

The Running Field

A few blocks away, tucked between old buildings, there was a small, run-down track.

Nothing special. Just a faded red running lane, a few metal bleachers, and a couple of flickering streetlights at the edges.

It wasn't locked up—just an open public field.

The perfect place to test his limits without getting caught.

Caleb scanned the area as he stepped onto the track.

Empty.

No people. No security. Just him and the wide-open space.

His heart pounded with anticipation.

Alright. Let's see what I can do.

The First Sprint

He took his place at the starting line, crouching slightly.

His muscles felt coiled, tense, ready.

Then—he pushed off.

And the world blurred.

The ground vanished beneath him, the wind slammed against his body, and before he even processed it—

He was halfway down the track.

His feet barely touched the ground before they pushed forward again. His arms pumped, his breath stayed steady.

He didn't just feel fast.

He felt untouchable.

His speed was unnatural.

Superhuman.

The Second Run: Pushing Limits

Caleb skidded to a stop at the end of the track, his breath steady, his heartbeat calm.

That was insane.

But he wasn't done.

He jogged back to the starting line, shaking out his limbs. Faster this time.

He crouched again.
This time, he focused.
Not just running—power. Acceleration.
Then—
He launched forward.
The world vanished around him.

The wind didn't just hit him—it roared past his ears. The track became a streak of color beneath him.

The end of the lane was seconds away.

He planted his foot and—stopped.

His body came to a perfect halt.

No stumble. No exhaustion.
Just pure control.
He let out a shaky breath.
I'm not just fast.
I'm something else entirely.

The Return to the Abandoned House

Caleb pulled his hood back up, slipping out of the track as quietly as he had come.

His mind raced as he made his way back to the abandoned house.

This wasn't just some weird reflex boost.

He was becoming something else.

And the scariest part?

He liked it.

A Chance at Survival

The sun hung low in the sky as Caleb walked along the cracked sidewalks, hands shoved into the pockets of his hoodie.

His clothes were worn, his sneakers scuffed, his hair a little messy from sleeping in an abandoned house. He didn't look bad, but he definitely looked out of place.

Like a kid with nowhere to be.

He had spent the last few days adjusting—bringing in supplies, testing his abilities, making the abandoned house feel like home.

But now, a new problem was creeping in.
Money.
Food wouldn't last forever. He needed a way to get something—even just a little.

The Store Owner

As he wandered past a small corner shop, a voice called out.

"Hey, kid!"

Caleb froze.

He turned to see an older man standing in the doorway, wiping his hands on a rag. The guy looked about in his sixties, dressed in a dusty apron, eyes sharp but not unkind.

"You need some work?" the man asked, nodding toward the store.

Caleb hesitated. "Uh... what?"

The man sighed, glancing him up and down. "You look like you could use a few bucks. You good at stocking shelves?"

Caleb blinked, caught off guard.

No questions. No asking where he was from. Just an offer.

He could've lied. Could've said he had somewhere to be.

But instead—he nodded.

"...Yeah. I can do that."

His First Job

The store was small, old, but packed with everything—from canned goods to hardware supplies.

The man—Mr. Lee, as he introduced himself—handed Caleb a broom first.

"Floor's a mess. Clean it up, and we'll see how you do."

Caleb didn't complain. He just got to work.

Sweeping. Stocking. Organizing shelves.

It was easy. Simple.

And for the first time in days, it felt normal.

After about an hour, Mr. Lee nodded in approval.

"You work fast," he muttered, counting out a few bills. "Here. That should get you a meal or two."

Caleb looked at the money. Not much—maybe ten bucks—but it was his.

Something about that felt different.

"Thanks," he said, tucking it away.

Mr. Lee studied him for a moment. "You from around here?"

Caleb hesitated, then shrugged. "Kinda."

The old man didn't push.

"Come back tomorrow," he said, heading toward the back. "I'll have more work if you want it."

Caleb nodded, something warm settling in his chest.

It wasn't much.

But it was a start.

Establishing Independence

For the next few days, Caleb returned to Mr. Lee's store every now and then.

Not every day—just enough to keep a little cash in his pocket.

He'd sweep floors, stock shelves, sometimes carry boxes from the back. Nothing special.

Mr. Lee never asked too many questions.

And Caleb never gave too many answers.

It was a quiet, unspoken agreement.

Caleb needed some cash.
Mr. Lee needed cheap labor.
That was it.

The Second Video That Changes Everything

The day had started like any other.

Caleb had woken up in his abandoned house, thrown on his hoodie, and made his way toward Mr. Lee's store for a few hours of work.

Nothing unusual. Nothing suspicious.

Just another day of pretending that his life was normal.

But today—that illusion would end.

The Incident: A Moment That Changes Everything

Caleb was crossing the street, hands in his pockets, mind elsewhere.

He wasn't paying attention.

Didn't even hear the car speeding around the corner.

The driver? Looking at their phone.

By the time Caleb sensed it, the car was already too close.

The moment slowed.

Instinct took over.
His muscles reacted before he even thought.
He twisted his body, pushing off the ground with impossible speed.
His feet barely touched the pavement before he vaulted over the car—clearing it completely.
He landed smoothly on the other side, his knees bending to absorb the impact.
A perfect, unnatural movement.
Something no human should be able to do.
The driver screamed, braking too late.

A few bystanders gasped, shouted.

And one?

One person had their phone up—recording.

The Video That Exposes Him

Within hours, the video was on social media.

"WTF did I just see?! This guy jumped over a freaking car!!!"

"This has to be fake... right???"

"Nah man, look at the way he moves... That ain't normal."

But then—someone else noticed.

A random commenter pulled up the first video—the one from the basketball court.

"Wait a sec... this is the SAME GUY from that reflex video. Look at the hoodie!"

And just like that...

The internet connected the dots.

Caleb wasn't just a random kid caught in an accident.

He was something else.

And now?

People were paying attention.

The Aftermath: Caleb Realizes He's Been Seen

Caleb sat in the backroom of Mr. Lee's shop, wiping sweat from his palms.

His mind raced.

He had seen the video.

People were talking.

Not just about the car jump. But about him.

They know.

Maybe not who he was.
Maybe not where he lived.

But they knew he existed.

And that meant...
Someone else might start looking.
Someone Starts Looking for Him

The video spread faster than Caleb expected.

Not viral in a global way—but enough.

Enough that the wrong kind of person saw it.

The Mysterious Figure

Somewhere in the city, in a dimly lit apartment, a man sat at his desk, staring at his screen.

His name didn't matter.

What mattered was that he had an eye for things that didn't make sense.

And this?

This didn't make sense.

He had seen the first video—the reflexes at the basketball court.

Dismissed it. Thought it was just a lucky reaction.

But now?

The car jump.
That wasn't luck. That wasn't normal.
He replayed the video, slowing it down.
The way the kid moved. The way he reacted before impact.
That was something else.
Something worth looking into.
He cracked his knuckles, leaning back.
Who are you, kid?
And more importantly...
Where are you hiding?

Caleb Realizes Someone Might Be Watching

Back at the abandoned house, Caleb sat on his old mattress, phone in hand, watching the comments flood in.

His foot tapped restlessly against the floor.

"This dude is unreal."

"Athlete? Parkour? Superhuman???"

"Anyone know where this happened?"

His stomach tightened.

They didn't know his name.
They didn't know his face clearly.
They didn't know where he was.

But they were asking questions.

And someone, somewhere...

Was looking for answers.

Caleb exhaled sharply, shutting off his phone.

I need to be more careful.

The feeling of being hunted had begun.

The Investigation Begins

The mysterious man sat in a dimly lit apartment, his laptop screen casting a cold glow on his face.

The video of Caleb's impossible jump played on loop.

Frame by frame.

Slowed down. Reversed. Analyzed.

His eyes narrowed.

Something in this video would tell him where it happened.

Breaking Down the Clues

He scanned the edges of the footage, looking beyond the action.

Ignoring the kid.

Focusing on the world around him.

-A blurry street sign in the background.
-A small store on the corner—part of the logo visible.
-The type of pavement markings—unique to certain parts of the city.

There.

Something familiar.

The man leaned closer, pausing the video.

That store.

He had seen it before.

He just needed to figure out where.

The First Step in the Hunt

He pulled up Google Maps, scrolling through the city.

If he could match the logo, the street layout, anything—he'd have a lead.

It wouldn't be instant.

It wouldn't be easy.

But it was a start.

And that was all he needed.

"I'll find you, kid."

Click. The video played again.
The Feeling of Being Watched
For the past few nights, Caleb had felt free.
Living alone, training his body, testing his limits.
But tonight?
Something felt wrong.

The First Hint

It started as a small thing.

A feeling. A slight unease in his chest.

Like the air around him had shifted.

He kept walking, hands stuffed in his hoodie pockets, trying to ignore it.

But then—

The distant click of a camera shutter.

The shuffle of footsteps that stopped when he did.

A shadow just out of view when he glanced over his shoulder.

No.

He was just being paranoid. Right?

Maybe it was just because of the video.

Maybe knowing that people were talking about him was making him jumpy.

Right?

Paranoia or Reality?

As he crossed the street, he tested it.

He walked a little faster.

His heartbeat picked up.

A cold wind rushed past him, rattling a street sign.

And then—

Footsteps.

Faster. Matching his pace.

Caleb turned the next corner sharply.

The street was empty.

Silent.
But that feeling?
It didn't go away.
He Knows Someone's Out There
Caleb exhaled slowly, forcing himself to stay calm.

Maybe it was nothing.
Maybe he was imagining it.
But deep down—
He knew.
Someone was looking for him.
And if he wasn't careful—
They were going to find him.

Someone Comes Asking Questions

Caleb was stacking shelves in the back of the small store, his mind elsewhere.

The uneasy feeling hadn't gone away.

Every night, it felt like someone was watching him.

Following him.

Maybe it was just paranoia.

But today?

Today, it became real.

The Man at the Front of the Store

The bell above the door jingled, and Caleb barely noticed—until he heard the voice.

Low. Controlled. Too calm.

"Excuse me."

Caleb froze.

Something about the tone sent a cold chill down his spine.

He moved silently, stepping closer to the wall, listening.

Mr. Lee was at the register, and Caleb could hear the quiet shuffle of a photo being placed on the counter.

"I'm looking for someone," the man said.

A pause.

"Have you seen him?"

Caleb's Heart Pounded

He didn't breathe.

Didn't move.

Because he knew.

Knew without looking that the picture was of him.

Mr. Lee's Answer

The silence stretched for a second too long.

Then—Mr. Lee's calm, unbothered voice.

"No. Haven't seen him."

Another pause.

Caleb gripped the shelf, his knuckles white.

The man hummed, like he wasn't sure if he believed it.

"You sure?"

"Yeah," Mr. Lee said easily. "Lots of kids pass through here. But this one? Haven't seen him."

The man exhaled.

"...Alright."

A quiet rustle—the picture being picked back up.

Then footsteps.

The bell jingled again.

And the man was gone.

Mr. Lee Confronts Caleb

For a few moments, Caleb didn't move.

Didn't breathe.

Then, slow footsteps made their way to the back.

Mr. Lee leaned against the doorway, arms crossed.

His expression was calm—but unreadable.

"You wanna tell me why some guy is showing me a picture of you?"

Caleb swallowed.

"I..."

Mr. Lee studied him.

Not angry. Not even suspicious.

But watching.

Waiting.

"...You in some kind of trouble, kid?"

Caleb Tries to Play It Off

Caleb forced a casual shrug, keeping his expression calm.

"No, Mr. Lee. Maybe it's just a misunderstanding."

His voice was steady, but inside?

His heart was pounding.

Mr. Lee didn't react at first. He just watched him.

Measured. Studied.

Then, after a long pause, he sighed.

"Yeah... maybe," he muttered, scratching his jaw. "But I've been around long enough to know when a kid's hiding something."

Caleb didn't flinch.

Didn't move.

Because he couldn't.

If he showed even the slightest sign of fear, Mr. Lee would see right through it.

The older man sighed again, rubbing the back of his neck.

"Well... whatever it is, just be careful," he finally said. "That guy wasn't just some lost tourist. He was looking for you."

Caleb nodded slowly.

"I will."

But as Mr. Lee walked away, the words echoed in his mind.

That guy was looking for you.

And for the first time, Caleb knew—

This wasn't just paranoia anymore.

It was real.

Someone was out there.

And if he wasn't careful—

They were going to find him.

The Event That Changes Everything

Caleb had been extra careful ever since Mr. Lee warned him.

He took different streets on his way to work. Stopped sneaking out as much.

But none of that mattered now.

Because today—everything was about to change.

The Accident: The Moment That Exposes Him

It happened so fast.

One second, Caleb was crossing the street.

The next—

 A car came speeding straight at him.

Too fast. No time to react.

The impact was brutal.

His body slammed against the windshield.

He was thrown into the air, flipping twice before crashing onto the pavement.

His shoes flew off—one landing near a bystander's feet.

For anyone else, that would've been the end.

But for Caleb?

Something impossible happened.

The Regeneration (All Caught on Camera)

The crowd gasped, shouted, phones already up, recording.

A woman screamed, "Oh my God, that kid is dead!"

But then—

Caleb moved.

His body twitched.

His breathing was normal.

And before their eyes—

His bones snapped back into place.
The bruises vanished.
The cuts sealed themselves instantly.

He sat up.

Completely fine.

The entire street was silent.

The Mark is Caught on Camera

Caleb's bare foot pressed against the pavement as he stood.
That's when someone noticed.
A close-up shot of his sole.
The mark.
Deep. Ancient-looking. Glowing faintly for a brief second.
"What... what is that?" someone muttered.
"Did you see that?!"
Click. Record. Post.
Within minutes—the video was online.

The Aftermath: The Whole World Sees Him

-The video spreads fast.

-People start analyzing it, questioning if it's real.

-Historians, archaeologists, and conspiracy theorists start noticing the mark.

-The mysterious man hunting Caleb sees it—and now he knows what to look for.

Caleb, panicked, disappears into the alleys, heart racing.

But it was too late.

The world had seen.

And now?

Everyone was looking for him.

Caleb Returns to the Abandoned House

Caleb's breath was still shaky as he sprinted through the alleyways.

The video. The mark. The way his body had healed in front of everyone.

They all saw it.

He turned corner after corner, cutting through empty lots, until finally—

He reached the abandoned house.

His only home.

But tonight, for the first time—

It didn't feel safe anymore.

Caleb Sees the Video Himself

He collapsed onto his mattress, grabbing his phone with trembling fingers.

His inbox was flooded with messages.

Even people he barely knew were sending links.

- "Dude, tell me this isn't you??"
- "WTF—this looks like that other video from a while back."
- "Yo... bro, I saw you DIE, and you just GOT UP?!?!"

Caleb's chest tightened.

He clicked the video.

And there he was.

The car hitting him.
The brutal impact.
His bones snapping... then fixing themselves instantly.

And then—

A zoomed-in shot of his foot.

The mark.

Its ancient, cryptic design was clear as day.

And worse?

People in the comments were already analyzing it.

How the Archaeologists Start Looking for Him

Some random history buff in the comments recognized the mark as Egyptian in origin.
A historian retweeted the video, asking: "Where was this recorded? Does anyone have more footage?"
An archaeologist specializing in ancient Egyptian symbols saw it... and recognized it instantly.

"This isn't just some random design."

"This is something we've been searching for."

"This kid is connected to it."

Now, they were looking.

And so was everyone else.

Alara Discovers the Video

The glow of the computer screen flickered in the dimly lit office.

Alara had been deep in research, scanning through old documents, analyzing symbols, piecing together history one artifact at a time.

She was used to working alone.

Used to long nights with nothing but books, maps, and the hum of her computer.

But tonight?

Tonight, her work was interrupted.

The Moment That Changed Everything

A notification popped up on her screen.

A trending video.

Something random. Something she would've ignored.

But then—

Her eyes locked onto the thumbnail.

A symbol.

Ancient. Familiar. Impossible.

She froze.

Heart pounding, she clicked the video—and everything changed.

Alara Watches in Shock

The footage played.

The accident. The impact.

The boy getting up—completely healed.

And then—

The mark on his foot.

Alara's breath caught in her throat.

She knew that symbol.

She had seen it before, buried in ancient texts.

It wasn't just a mark.

It was a legacy. A calling.

Something that wasn't supposed to exist anymore.

Yet here it was.

And this boy—he had it.

The Realization

Her fingers hovered over the keyboard, trembling.

She should've dismissed it.

Should've told herself it was fake.

But deep down, she knew the truth.

This was real.

And she was going to find him.

Alara Calls a Historian Friend

Alara couldn't stop staring at the screen.

The video kept playing on loop—Caleb's impossible recovery, the ancient mark on his foot.

Her mind raced.

This wasn't just another internet hoax.

This was something real.

And she knew exactly who to call.

The Call to a Historian Friend

She grabbed her phone, scrolling through contacts until she found the name.
Dr. Ethan Carter – Historian, researcher, and one of the few people she actually trusted.
The phone rang twice before his familiar voice answered.
"Alara? This is a surprise. You never call unless it's urgent."
She didn't waste time.
"Ethan. I need you to watch something. Right now."

There was a pause. Then a sigh. "Alright, what am I looking at?"
She sent the link.
A few seconds of silence.
Then—his voice changed.
"What the hell did I just watch?"
Ethan's Reaction

She could hear him rewinding the video, watching it again.
Then—his tone sharpened.
"Alara... that mark. Tell me you're seeing what I'm seeing."
She swallowed hard. "I saw it the second the video started."
"No. No way. This can't be real."
But he didn't sound skeptical.
He sounded intrigued.
And maybe even... a little scared.

The History Behind the Mark

"Ethan," she pressed, "You've studied ancient Egyptian symbols longer than I have. This mark—it's familiar, isn't it?"

He was quiet for a moment. Then—

"Not just familiar. It's identical to something I saw in an old manuscript years ago. Something that was supposed to be a myth."

Her heart pounded.

"You're telling me this kid—this random boy in the middle of nowhere—is connected to an ancient legend?"

A slow exhale from Ethan.

"Alara... I think we need to find him. Before someone else does."

The Story Hits International News

Breaking News – "The Miracle Boy" Goes Global

The internet exploded overnight.

The video of the mysterious boy surviving a deadly car accident and instantly healing had now spread across every major news outlet.

CNN LIVE – "A Hoax or a Medical Mystery?"

"Tonight, a shocking video is going viral across the globe. A teenage boy in an undisclosed location appears to survive a brutal car accident... and, incredibly, heals within seconds."

"Many are calling it a hoax, but experts are divided."

A clip of the accident played on loop in the corner of the screen.

"There's no way this is real," a skeptical guest argued. "This is just clever editing."

"Then explain the eyewitness accounts," the host challenged.

"People will believe anything they see online," another guest scoffed. "Look, it's probably some viral stunt. This 'kid' is probably an actor."

"But what about the symbol on his foot?"

The screen cut to a zoomed-in image of Caleb's mark.

BBC News – "Could This Be a Genetic Mutation?"

"A debate is unfolding in the scientific community regarding the authenticity of the so-called 'Miracle Boy' video. While skeptics argue it is a hoax, some medical experts suggest that, if real, this could indicate an advanced form of human regeneration."

An expert in genetics appeared on the screen.

"There are known cases of rapid healing due to genetic mutations, but nothing—nothing—at this level."

"Are you suggesting this boy is an evolutionary anomaly?" the anchor asked.

The scientist hesitated. "If this is real, then we are looking at something unprecedented."

Egyptian News Channel – "An Ancient Connection?"

But then—the conversation changed.

The story had reached Egypt.

And that's when things became even stranger.

An Egyptian historian appeared on live television, holding an ancient manuscript.

"This symbol... it has not been seen for thousands of years."

"What do you mean?" the news anchor asked, intrigued.

The historian flipped through the old texts, revealing a faded drawing of a similar mark.

"This symbol was associated with something believed to be a myth—the legacy of the forgotten pharaohs. A lost bloodline."

"And you're saying this boy… could be linked to that?"

The historian leaned forward.

"I am saying… we must find out."

X & Social Media Explode

* #MiracleBoy trends worldwide.
* Conspiracy theories flood the internet—"Is this a secret government experiment?"
* Debates spark: "Real or Fake?"
* Memes take over: "The first superhero reveal??"

But beneath the chaos, a new discussion begins.

Who is this boy?

And more importantly…

Where is he?

Caleb Returns to Mr. Lee

Caleb kept his hood up, moving quickly through the city streets.

His face was everywhere.

He had seen the news.

The entire world was talking about him.

And he had nowhere to go.

But right now, he needed something.

Something from Mr. Lee's shop.

Maybe food. Maybe cash. Maybe just a moment to breathe.

The Conversation with Mr. Lee

The bell jingled as Caleb stepped inside the store.

Mr. Lee was behind the counter, reading a newspaper, but the moment he looked up—

He froze.

Then, with a smirk, he folded the paper, tossing it aside.

"Damn, boy, I didn't know I hired an alien."

Caleb exhaled sharply, rubbing his forehead. "Not you too, Mr. Lee."

Mr. Lee chuckled, leaning on the counter.

"You wanna explain how you got hit by a car, got up like it was nothing, and now you're on every damn news channel?"

Caleb hesitated.

What could he say?

That he had no idea what was happening to him?
That he wished he could take it all back?
That now, he was being hunted?

Instead, he just muttered, "I don't know, okay? I just... I didn't ask for any of this."

Mr. Lee studied him for a long moment.

Then, finally, he sighed. "You need anything?"

Caleb hesitated, then nodded. "Just some supplies."

Mr. Lee grabbed a paper bag, filling it up without asking questions.

As he handed it over, he met Caleb's gaze.

"You better be careful, kid. The world's looking for you now. And not all of them are gonna be friendly."

Caleb swallowed hard. "I know."

And with that, he turned and walked out.

The Chase Begins: Caleb is Not Alone

As soon as Caleb stepped onto the sidewalk, the feeling hit him.

That creeping sensation.

That chill down his spine.

Someone was watching him.

He started walking faster.

Then—a noise.

A sharp movement from across the street.

Caleb's breath hitched. He turned his head just slightly.

And there—standing in the shadows—

The man.

The same man who had been asking about him.

The man who had been looking for him.

And now—he had found him.

Caleb Runs for His Life

The man moved.

Caleb's body reacted before his mind could.

He ran.

- His feet hit the pavement hard, fast, faster than any normal human.
- He weaved through traffic, dodging cars effortlessly.
- He heard the man following—keeping up.

But Caleb was faster.
Way faster.
He turned sharply, cutting into an alleyway.
Then another.
Then—he jumped.
Scaling a fence in seconds, flipping over it like it was nothing.
By the time he landed on the other side—

- The man was gone.
- The street was silent.
- He was alone again.

Heart racing, Caleb exhaled sharply.
That was too close.
And now he knew—
Whoever that man was, he wasn't just watching anymore.
He was chasing.
And next time?
Caleb might not get away.

Alara & Ethan Plan Their Search

The air in Alara's office was tense. Papers were scattered across the desk, the glow of the laptop screen illuminating the paused frame of the video—the one that had changed everything.

Caleb.

The mark.

The impossible healing.

And now?

The entire world was looking for him.

Alara & Ethan's Plan to Find Caleb

Ethan leaned back, rubbing his temples. "Okay, let's go over what we know."

Alara sighed, pulling up a map of the city. "We know this footage is real. We know the symbol on his foot isn't just random—it has connections to ancient Egypt."

Ethan nodded. "And we know he's hiding."

Alara exhaled sharply. "That's the problem, Ethan. This kid is probably scared out of his mind. He doesn't know who to trust, and with the entire world chasing him, if the wrong people find him first..."

She didn't finish.

They both knew the stakes.

The Plan: Finding Caleb Before Someone Else Does

◆ Step One: Pinpoint His Location

They analyzed the background in the video.

A shop sign. A familiar street.

Cross-referencing news reports, Ethan narrowed it down to a specific area of the city.

◆ Step Two: Find Someone Who's Seen Him

A kid on the run doesn't live off nothing.

He had to be getting food, supplies, shelter.

They needed to find a store owner, a worker—someone who had seen him.

◆ Step Three: Get to Him First

Before the government.

Before the mysterious man.

Before anyone else who might want to use him.

Mr. Lee Becomes a Key Lead

Ethan squinted at a small detail in the video's background.

A familiar storefront.

He froze.

"Alara... I know that shop."

Alara frowned, leaning closer. "You do?"

Ethan nodded. "I used to live in this city for a while. That's a corner shop—owned by an older guy. I think his name is... Mr. Lee."

Alara grabbed her coat. "Then we need to talk to him. Now."

Scene: Alara & Ethan Confront Mr. Lee

The bell jingled as they entered the store.

Mr. Lee was restocking shelves, humming to himself—until he saw them.

His eyes narrowed.

He didn't like strangers asking questions.

Especially about Caleb.

Ethan stepped forward first. "Excuse me, sir. We need to ask you about someone."

Mr. Lee sighed, crossing his arms. "If it's about that 'miracle boy' nonsense, I ain't interested."

Alara placed a photo of the mark on the counter. "Please. We just need to know if you've seen him."

His jaw tightened.

Silence.

Then, finally, Mr. Lee muttered: "Why?"

Alara leaned in.

Her voice was low, urgent.

"Because if we don't find him first, someone else will. And they might not have good intentions."

Mr. Lee studied them for a long moment.

Then he exhaled. "Damn it, kid."

Mr. Lee Gives Them a Lead

Mr. Lee let out a long sigh, rubbing the back of his neck. "Damn it, kid... you're making me do more talking than I usually like."

Alara and Ethan watched him carefully, waiting for his answer.

Finally, Mr. Lee placed both hands on the counter and met their gaze.

"Yeah. He was here earlier today."

Alara's Heart Skipped a Beat

Ethan leaned in. "You're sure?"

Mr. Lee scoffed. "Hard to forget a kid who got hit by a car, healed like magic, and now has the whole damn world looking for him."

Alara and Ethan exchanged glances. They were so close.

But then—Mr. Lee's expression darkened.

"And you're not the only ones looking for him."

Ethan's Stomach Dropped

"Who?" Ethan asked quickly. "Who else is after him?"

Mr. Lee frowned, shaking his head. "Some guy. Tall, serious-looking. The kind of guy who doesn't ask questions—he demands answers."

Alara's grip on the counter tightened.

The mysterious man.

The one Caleb had already outrun.

That meant whoever he was... he was closing in too.

Does Mr. Lee Know Where Caleb Is?

Alara took a deep breath. "Do you know where he's staying?"

Mr. Lee hesitated.

He wasn't the type to give away a kid's secrets.

But he also wasn't the type to let a kid get caught by the wrong people.

"He didn't tell me much," he admitted. "Didn't trust anyone enough for that."

Ethan frowned. "But he must've mentioned something."

Mr. Lee rubbed his chin, thinking.

Then—his eyes flickered with a memory.

"He said something about living on the edge of the city. In an abandoned house."

Alara and Ethan locked eyes.

That was all they needed.

The Race to Find Caleb First Begins

- Alara & Ethan now have a real lead.
- The mysterious man is also searching—and might be ahead of them.
- Caleb, still unaware of how close they are, is running out of time.

A Dangerous Encounter

Alara and Ethan moved quickly through the streets, heading toward the outskirts of the city.

They were so close.

If they could just get to Caleb first, before anyone else—

But fate had other plans.

Inside a Small Store... A Dangerous Presence

They had stopped at a corner store, grabbing water and a map before heading out.

Alara stood by the register, focused on her phone, scanning online forums where people were still debating Caleb's existence.

Ethan was by the shelves, grabbing a pack of gum, his mind racing.

Neither of them noticed the man enter the store.

But the moment he spoke, a chill ran through Alara's spine.

The Mysterious Man Speaks

His voice was calm. Too calm.

"Excuse me."

The cashier looked up. "Yeah?"

The man pulled out his phone, showing a paused frame of the video—Caleb's face.

"I'm looking for this boy. Have you seen him?"

Alara's stomach dropped.

She didn't turn around. Didn't move.

But she knew.

Knew that the man standing just a few feet away wasn't just another curious stranger.

He was one of them.

Someone else hunting Caleb.

And now, they were breathing the same air.

Ethan Notices... and Reacts First

From the corner of his eye, Ethan saw Alara stiffen.

That was all it took for him to understand.

He didn't hesitate.

He grabbed a random item from the shelf and turned, bumping into Alara—forcing her to move.

"C'mon, we're late." His voice was normal, but his eyes were sharp. Warning her.

Alara nodded quickly, catching on.

They moved toward the exit casually—but fast.

Not running.

But not staying a second longer.

The man barely glanced at them.

But as they left, Alara couldn't shake the feeling—

That he had noticed them, too.

Once Outside: A Realization

They didn't speak until they had turned two corners, disappearing into the streets.

Then—Alara finally exhaled.

"That was him."

Ethan nodded grimly.

"He's hunting Caleb too."

Alara's fists clenched. "Then we need to move. Now."

Because now, it wasn't just about finding Caleb.

It was about getting to him before the wrong people did.

Caleb Feels the Pressure Closing In

Caleb sat on the old mattress in the abandoned house, the dim glow of his phone screen illuminating his face.

He had stopped checking the news.

Stopped reading the comments on the viral video.

None of it mattered anymore.

Because deep down, he knew—

They were coming for him.

The Feeling of Being Hunted

Every small noise outside made his chest tighten.

Every gust of wind, every distant footstep felt like a sign that someone was near.

And the worst part?

He didn't know who.

Was it the man who had chased him earlier?
Was it the government, finally closing in?
Or was it someone else entirely?

All he knew was one thing—

He couldn't stay here much longer.

A Critical Decision: Stay or Run?

His mind raced.

Stay in the abandoned house – It was dangerous, but at least he knew the area.

Run before it's too late – But where? He had nowhere to go.

His fingers tightened around the fabric of his hoodie.

The mark on his foot felt warm, almost as if it knew something was about to happen.

Alara & Ethan Close In

The car moved slowly along the empty road, its headlights cutting through the darkness.

Alara sat in the passenger seat, eyes scanning every abandoned structure they passed.

Ethan gripped the steering wheel, his jaw tight with concentration.

"There are too many empty buildings out here," he muttered. "If he's hiding in one of these, we'll be searching all night."

Alara leaned forward, studying the surroundings. "No. We're close—I can feel it."

But they needed something.

Some kind of sign.

And then—

She saw it.

The Light in the Darkness

At first, it was nothing.

Just another dark, decaying house on the edge of the city.

No lights. No movement.

But then—a flicker.

Something inside.

A faint glow. Not enough to be a full light source, but enough to suggest that someone was in there.

Ethan slowed the car, following Alara's gaze.

"You see that?"

Alara nodded slowly.

"Yeah... I do."

They Make Their Move

The car rolled to a stop a short distance away.

Alara and Ethan stepped out, their boots crunching against the gravel road.

Ethan clicked on a flashlight, its bright beam cutting through the night.
The house looked ancient, forgotten.
But the faint light inside was proof enough—
Someone was here.
Someone was hiding.
And they both knew exactly who it was.
As They Approach, Caleb Hears Them
Inside the abandoned house, Caleb sat frozen.

The sound of car doors closing.

Then—footsteps.

Two voices.

Talking. Outside.

His heart pounded.

Were they here to take him?
Were they part of the government? The man from earlier?
He held his breath, listening.
Outside, Alara & Ethan Speak
"This could be it," Ethan whispered, scanning the house with his flashlight.
Alara nodded. "Yeah... I think we found him."

The Choice: Stay or Leave?

Inside, Caleb's chest tightened.

Caleb Makes the Choice

Inside the abandoned house, Caleb's heart pounded.

He knew he couldn't run forever.

The streets weren't safe. Nowhere was safe.

And these people—they knew about the mark.

They weren't just random strangers.

They knew who he was.

Maybe even more than he did.

The Tension Before the First Contact

The night was silent except for the occasional whisper of the wind through the cracked wooden panels of the abandoned house.

Alara and Ethan stood outside the door, their flashlight beams cutting through the darkness.

The house was old—falling apart, forgotten.

But there was something about it.

Something that made Alara's gut tell her they had found the right place.

She took a step forward, her boots crunching softly against the dirt.

Ethan glanced at her. "You sure about this?"

Alara took a slow breath. "Only one way to find out."

She raised a hand—paused.

Then knocked.

Three times.

Inside, Caleb Froze

The knocks echoed through the empty space, bouncing off the old walls.

His breath hitched.

They had found him.

But who were they?

Outside, Alara Calls Out

"Hello? Is anyone in there?"

Her voice was gentle, but firm enough to be heard.

No response.

She glanced at Ethan.

Then tried again.

"Look, we don't mean any harm. If someone's in there... we just want to talk."

Still—silence.

But she could feel it.

Someone was listening.

Inside, Caleb's Heart Raced

They weren't forcing their way in.

They weren't shouting.

But they weren't leaving either.

He pressed his back against the wall, fists clenched.

His body was tense, ready to run—but something kept him still.

Something about the woman's voice.

She didn't sound like the people he had been running from.

Ethan Steps Closer

Ethan cleared his throat, lowering his voice.

"Listen... We know you're in there. We're not here to turn you in. We just want to help."

Alara added, "We know what's happening to you. We know about the mark."

Caleb's eyes widened.

They knew about the mark?

The Choice: Does Caleb Reveal Himself?

His breath shook.

His mind raced.

Stay hidden and hope they leave?
Run now before it's too late?
Or step forward... and hear what they have to say?

His fingers twitched.

His body burned with tension.

This was it.

The moment that would change everything.

Caleb's Inner Battle

Caleb pressed his back against the cold wall, his breathing shallow.

The voices outside were calm, steady.

They weren't yelling orders.

They weren't forcing their way in.

But that didn't mean they weren't dangerous.

Caleb Talks to Himself

His fingers twitched against his hoodie as he whispered to himself.

"Maybe this is my chance..."

He swallowed hard, staring at the door.

"Maybe they really do know about the mark... about what's happening to me."

His eyes flickered down to his foot—the mark burned against his skin, like it was pulsing in anticipation.

A reminder that he wasn't normal anymore.

That he had never been normal.

His vision sharpened, cutting through the shadows of the room.

Every crack in the wood, every speck of dust floating in the air—he saw it all, perfectly.

He could see in complete darkness.

A new ability... another mystery.

Something that they might have answers to.

He clenched his fists.
Was this the right choice?

Or was he walking into another trap?

Outside, Alara & Ethan Wait

Alara's breath formed a small cloud in the cold night air.

She glanced at Ethan, her expression tense.

"What if he doesn't trust us?"

Ethan sighed. "Then we're back to square one."

Then—

A voice.

Low. Careful. From inside.

Caleb Speaks From Behind the Door

"How can I be sure you're telling the truth?"

Alara's eyes widened slightly.

Ethan let out a breath.

Finally.

"Because we know what's happening to you," Alara answered, stepping closer to the door.

"The mark on your foot—it's not random. It's not just some symbol. It's connected to something ancient."

Caleb's heart pounded.

He pressed his fingers against the door.

"What do you mean?"

Ethan spoke next, keeping his voice even, measured.

"That mark has been hidden in history for thousands of years. We've only seen it in ancient texts, on lost artifacts. But never—never—on a living person."

Alara's voice softened.

"You're not just some random kid, Caleb. That mark means something. And we want to help you understand it."

Caleb's Decision

Silence.

Caleb's breath shook.

This was it.

This was the moment he had to choose—

Stay hidden, keep running, trust no one?
Or take the risk... and find out the truth?

He exhaled slowly.

His fingers wrapped around the door handle.

Then—

The door creaked open.

A sliver of dim light from the moon spilled inside.

Alara and Ethan stood just outside, their faces lit only by the glow of the flashlight.

Caleb's sharp night vision allowed him to see every detail—their uncertain expressions, the tension in their stance, the breath forming in the cold air.

He studied them. Analyzed them.
Then, finally—
He stepped forward.

The First Conversation

The old wooden door creaked open, revealing the two strangers standing outside.

Caleb studied them carefully, his sharp vision picking up every small detail—the way the woman's hands were steady, but her eyes searched him like she was figuring him out.

The man behind her had a more guarded stance, like he was ready for anything.

They weren't threatening.

But they weren't fully safe, either.

Slowly, they stepped inside.

Inside the Abandoned House

The flashlight beam moved across the room, revealing cracked walls, an old mattress, and scattered supplies.

Alara glanced around. "This is where you've been staying?"

Her voice wasn't judging. Just... surprised.

The boy didn't answer.

Ethan exhaled, looking around the space. "Not exactly home sweet home, huh?"

Still, silence.

The boy just watched them, his posture tense.

The First Questions

Alara took a small step closer, keeping her voice soft.

"What's your name?"

A pause.

The boy hesitated.

Then—finally—he answered.

"Caleb."

Alara nodded, filing the name away.

"Do you have family, Caleb? Someone looking for you?"

His jaw tightened.

Then, quietly—"No."

Ethan and Alara exchanged a look.

No family. No one looking for him.

That meant he was truly alone.

Which also meant...

He had nowhere else to go.

Convincing Him to Leave

Alara took a deep breath.

"Listen, Caleb... I know you don't trust us. And you don't have to. But what you do have to know is—this place isn't safe anymore."

Caleb's fists clenched slightly.

Ethan nodded. "You're on every news channel. You know that, right?"

Caleb looked away, frustration flickering in his eyes.

"I know."

"Then you also know," Alara added, "that it's only a matter of time before the wrong people find you."

Caleb's heartbeat picked up.

Because deep down—he knew they were right.

The Offer

Alara's voice softened.

"We have a safer place for you. Somewhere they won't find you."

Ethan crossed his arms. "You can stay here, keep hiding, keep running... but that won't last much longer. Or you can come with us."

Caleb's chest tightened.

He didn't fully trust them.

But...

Wasn't this better than running alone?

He took a shaky breath.

Then—finally—he nodded.

"Fine. I'll go with you."

But his eyes—

They told a different story.

He wasn't fully convinced.

Not yet.

The Suspicious Car

The night air felt colder as they stepped outside.

The abandoned house stood silent behind them, but the moment they reached the edge of the yard—

Alara froze.

Ethan followed her gaze, his stomach dropping.

A car.

Sitting just down the street, headlights on, engine idling quietly.

It wasn't too close.

But it wasn't far enough to be a coincidence.

The Urgency Kicks In

"Get in the car. Now." Ethan's voice was low, firm.

Caleb hesitated. "What's wrong?"

Alara didn't answer. She just grabbed his arm and pulled him toward their vehicle.

Her gut screamed danger.

Ethan slid into the driver's seat, gripping the wheel. "Let's not wait to find out who they are."

Alara barely had time to buckle up before—

VROOOOM.

The car lurched forward, speeding down the road.

They're Being Followed

Alara glanced in the side mirror.

The car behind them moved too.

Same speed. Same direction.

"Sh*t." She exhaled sharply. "They're following us."

Caleb's pulse spiked.

"Who are they?"

Ethan's jaw clenched. "I don't know. But we're about to find out."

The Full-Blown Chase Begins

The tires screeched against the pavement as Ethan pressed the gas.

The car lurched forward, speeding down the dark road.

Behind them—

The suspicious car accelerated too.

Alara gripped the dashboard. "They're speeding up."

Caleb turned in his seat, his night vision cutting through the darkness. He saw the silhouette of the driver—but not their face.

His stomach twisted. Who was chasing them?

The Chase Intensifies

VROOM!

The car behind them gained speed, closing the distance.

Ethan's hands were tight on the wheel.

"Hold on!"

He took a sharp turn—tires screeching, dust kicking up behind them.

The car behind them followed, not letting up.

Alara cursed under her breath. "They're not just following. They know who we are."

Caleb's pulse pounded in his ears.

They weren't getting away that easily.

Narrow Escape Through the City

The road ahead split into two paths.

One led to the main highway—too exposed.
The other—narrow side streets.

"Left! Take the side streets!" Alara shouted.

Ethan yanked the wheel, barely missing a streetlight as they swerved into the tighter roads.

The buildings around them blurred past.

For a second— Caleb thought they had lost them.

But then—

Headlights reappeared behind them.

"Dammit, they're still on us!" Ethan growled.

Caleb Feels Something... A New Ability?

Caleb's head started buzzing.

A strange sensation pulsed through his body.

His vision sharpened, his senses stretched outward.

For a brief moment—he could almost feel the driver behind them.

A presence. A focus.

Like he could predict their next move.

He clenched his fists.

What is happening to me?

Final Move: Losing the Pursuers

Ethan gritted his teeth.

"Alright, let's end this."

He spotted an upcoming alleyway. Narrow. Barely wide enough for a car.

"Hold on!"

He cut the wheel—hard.

The car skidded sideways, narrowly squeezing through the tight gap.

Behind them—

The pursuing car couldn't make the turn in time.

TIRES SCREECHED.

The driver tried to brake, but—

CRASH!

Their car slammed into a row of dumpsters, knocking over metal and debris.

Smoke rose from the hood.

Ethan didn't wait to see if they recovered.

He gunned the accelerator—and they disappeared into the night.

They're Safe... For Now.
The car slowed as they finally reached a quiet road.
Silence filled the air.
Everyone was catching their breath.
Caleb's hands were shaking slightly.
Alara turned in her seat, looking at him.
"Welcome to our world."
Caleb exhaled, looking at her—
And for the first time, he realized...
He was in something bigger than he ever imagined.

Arriving at the Secret Research Location

The car sped down the empty highway, the tension still thick in the air from the chase.

Ethan gripped the wheel tightly, checking the mirrors every few minutes to make sure they weren't being followed again.

Alara glanced back at Caleb, who was staring out the window, his mind a storm of thoughts.

He had escaped.

But he wasn't free.
And now, he was being taken to a place he knew nothing about.

Caleb Finally Speaks

After a long silence, Caleb's voice cut through the dark car interior.

"Where are we going?"
Alara turned toward him. "Somewhere safe. A place where we can start answering your questions."
Ethan exhaled. "And where you won't have to sleep on a filthy mattress in an abandoned house."
Caleb frowned slightly. "You still haven't told me why you're helping me."
Alara hesitated. Then—"Because we've spent years looking for someone like you. And we never thought we'd find you."
That didn't make Caleb feel any better.
He pulled his hoodie tighter, his mind racing.

The Hidden Facility

An hour later, they reached a remote, unmarked road, surrounded by thick woods.

Ethan pulled up to what looked like an old industrial warehouse, abandoned like everything else in Caleb's life.

"This is your big research facility?" Caleb muttered.
Ethan smirked. "Not everything is what it looks like."
Alara pulled out a small key card and swiped it against a rusted panel on the side of the door.
At first, nothing happened.
Then—a faint beep.
Gears turned.
And with a loud hiss, the door slid open, revealing a staircase leading underground.
Caleb's breath caught.

"Whoa."

Alara gestured forward. "Welcome to the place where history and secrets collide."

Inside the Underground Lab

The facility was far more advanced than Caleb expected.

The underground space was clean, modern, lined with glass walls and holographic screens displaying ancient symbols, texts, and maps.
Research equipment, computers, and even a few old artifacts were spread throughout the large space.
Everything was connected to one thing. Him. Or more specifically—his mark.

Caleb Finally Asks About His Mark

Caleb swallowed hard, his fingers unconsciously touching the sole of his foot where the mark still burned slightly.

He turned to Alara, his voice quieter now.

"What is this?"

Alara and Ethan exchanged a look.

Then—Alara took a deep breath and said the words that would change everything.

"It's the mark of a forgotten bloodline. A lineage that was never supposed to survive."

Caleb's heartbeat slammed in his chest.

He clenched his fists.

"What does that mean?"

Alara's gaze locked onto him.

"It means you're not just a boy, Caleb. You're a part of something ancient... something powerful. And now that you've been found—the world will never be the same again."

The Hidden Text That Describes Caleb

The research facility is eerily quiet. The hum of machines fills the air, but the vast, dimly lit archives feel untouched by time. Alara and Dr. Ethan Carter lead Caleb down a corridor lined with ancient books, scrolls, and sealed artifacts.

Caleb, still confused about why these people took him in, keeps his distance. He doesn't trust them yet.

Finally, they enter a secure study room, where an old manuscript lies carefully displayed on a large oak table. The pages are yellowed, fragile—clearly ancient.

Dr. Ethan, adjusting his glasses, flips through the delicate pages. His fingers stop at a passage, and he exhales.

> "The child of the lost bloodline... a survivor, marked by the serpent, hidden from time."

Caleb's breath catches in his throat. The words feel like they're speaking directly to him.

Alara leans forward, watching Caleb's reaction. "Caleb... this was written centuries ago. There's no way it should describe you so perfectly. But it does."

Ethan continues, his voice steady but fascinated.

> "He who bears the mark shall awaken in an age not his own.
> His blood will stir, and the lost throne shall call to him.
> He will walk among men, but not as one of them.
> The serpent's will guides him.
> He is the key... or the curse."

Silence.

Caleb stares at the text, his hands clenched. His mind is racing.

> "This doesn't mean anything." He steps back. "It's just some old story, right?"

But Alara and Ethan don't answer.

They know it's more than that.

The Vision in the Desert

After hearing the text that describes him, Caleb's heart pounds in his chest. He feels something... stirring inside him.

> "What does this mean?" he asks, his voice lower now, almost afraid of the answer.

Dr. Ethan removes his glasses, rubbing his temples.

> "We found this text in a place that shouldn't exist, Caleb. A hidden chamber—beneath the Great Pyramid of Giza."

Caleb freezes. The pyramids?

> "There were no doors, no tunnels leading to it. Just a sealed-off chamber... as if it had been hidden on purpose."

His vision blurs. The words feel too heavy, too real—like they are pulling him somewhere he can't control.

Suddenly—
Darkness.

Inside the Vision

Caleb is standing in the desert.

The air is warm, dry. The sand beneath his feet feels real—too real. He looks up, and there, standing tall and eternal, are the pyramids of Egypt. Their golden stones glow under the sun, as if untouched by time.

But something is wrong.

He hears voices. Faint at first, then growing clearer.

He turns—

And he sees them.

A grand palace rises from the sands, surrounded by figures in golden robes and crowns. The pharaohs. Their faces are solemn, powerful, their eyes filled with something ancient and knowing.

And in the middle of them... A child.

Dressed in royal garments, with a golden serpent on his arm. He laughs, carefree, playing in the sand, unaware of the weight of his fate.

One of the pharaohs kneels before the child, placing a hand on his shoulder. His voice is deep, commanding, yet filled with warmth.

> "My son... the one who will last for centuries.
The one whom time will not take.
And when the time comes...
The serpent will come for you."

The wind howls, the sand rises like a storm—

And suddenly—

Caleb wakes up.

Back in the Facility – Caleb's Shock

Caleb jerks back in his chair, breathing hard. His hands are shaking. The room is spinning.

Alara and Ethan rush toward him.

> "Caleb?!" Alara grips his shoulder. "What happened?"

He looks at her, then at Ethan.

> "I... I saw something."
"The pyramids. The pharaohs. A child." He hesitates, his voice shaking.

"They called me... my son."

Silence.

Alara and Ethan exchange a glance. They don't know what to say.

> "What does this mean?" Caleb whispers.

And for the first time, Dr. Ethan Carter—the historian, the skeptic—looks truly afraid.

Caleb Thinks He's Losing His Mind

The research facility feels colder now. Or maybe it's just Caleb.

He grips the edge of the table, his knuckles white. His breathing is uneven, his mind spinning.

> "No, no, no…" he mutters under his breath, shaking his head. "That wasn't real."

But the images won't leave him.

The pyramids. The sand. The voices. The child the pharaohs called 'my son.'

He presses his palms against his forehead, squeezing his eyes shut. His pulse pounds in his ears.
> "I'm losing my mind." His voice is barely above a whisper.

Alara's Reaction – Trying to Comfort Him

Alara watches him, unsure of what to do.

She's never seen him like this. He was already shaken when they found him, but this? This is something deeper.

She slowly reaches out, placing a careful hand on his arm.

> "Caleb… just breathe, okay?" Her voice is soft, steady. "You're not crazy."

He lets out a sharp laugh—bitter, almost broken.

> "Oh, really?" He lifts his head, eyes locking onto hers. "Because I just had a full-on hallucination of ancient Egypt."

Alara hesitates.

Because a part of her agrees with him. It shouldn't be possible.

But something about this… doesn't feel like just a hallucination.

> "Maybe it means something." She swallows. "What if—"

> "No." Caleb pulls away from her touch. "I don't want to hear 'maybe.' I want the truth. I want to wake up and not feel like I'm..."

His voice cracks. He stops himself, jaw tightening.

> "...breaking."

Ethan's Response – Logic vs Fear

Dr. Ethan Carter has been silent. Watching. Analyzing. But something about what Caleb said—what he saw—unsettles him.

> "Tell me everything you saw." His voice is calm, but there's a sharp edge to it.

Caleb doesn't answer right away. He doesn't want to relive it.

But Alara, sensing that maybe Ethan can help, gently pushes.

> "Caleb..." She meets his eyes. "Just tell us."

Caleb exhales slowly. His hands are still shaking.

> "I was in the desert. The pyramids were there, but it didn't feel like now. It felt... ancient."

Ethan leans in, listening carefully.

> "I heard voices," Caleb continues, his own voice distant. "There were pharaohs. Princes. People in golden robes. And a kid..." He hesitates, then mutters, "...a kid they called their son."

Ethan's expression darkens. His fingers drum against the table.

> "And they said...?"

Caleb doesn't want to say it. But the words echo in his head like a ghost.

> "...'My son. The one who will last for centuries. And when the time comes, the serpent will come for you.'"

Silence.

Ethan stares at him. Alara's grip on the table tightens.

Because this isn't normal.

This shouldn't be happening.

And yet... it is.

Alara's Growing Belief – Is This More Than Coincidence?

Alara can see the fear in Caleb's eyes. She wants to believe this is just some weird episode—that he's just exhausted, that everything will make sense soon.
But deep down... she feels it.
> This isn't just a coincidence.

Not after what they found in the ancient text.
Not after Caleb's mark.
Not after the undiscovered chamber beneath the pyramid.
Her scientific mind tells her to be rational.

But her gut tells her something bigger is happening.

She finally speaks, her voice softer now.

> "Caleb... what if this isn't just in your head?"

He looks up at her, his eyes tired, searching.

> "What if..." she hesitates, but then forces herself to say it. "...what if this is real?"

Alara & Ethan's Private Conversation – The Decision to Protect Caleb

After Caleb's vision, he's still shaken. His mind is spinning, and he doesn't want to hear more. He pulls away from them, muttering that he needs a moment alone.

Alara and Ethan exchange a look.

They step out of the room, moving into a quiet hallway of the research facility. The air feels heavy.

> Alara runs a hand through her hair, exhaling sharply.
"What do I tell you, Ethan?" She turns to face him. "If this is real... if Caleb is really connected to all of this—then we have to protect him. At any cost."

Ethan removes his glasses, rubbing his forehead.
> "You're saying that like we even know what we're protecting him from." His voice is tired, but there's an edge to it.

Alara crosses her arms, staring at him.
> "We don't. But that doesn't change the fact that he's in danger."
Ethan exhales, shaking his head.

> "Alara, we are scientists. Historians. Researchers. We are not protectors. We are not soldiers."
> "Then we become them." Her voice is firm, unwavering.
Ethan looks at her—really looks at her.

Because Alara isn't scared.

She's determined.

And that scares him more than anything.

Ethan's Hesitation – The Weight of What This Means

Ethan sighs, his fingers gripping the bridge of his nose.

> "Do you hear yourself?" He keeps his voice low, not wanting Caleb to hear. "This isn't just an old myth anymore. This is something dangerous. Something we can't explain."

> Alara steps closer. "Exactly. Which means someone else already knows. And if they know, they'll come for him."

Ethan clenches his jaw.

Because she's right.

> "...If we do this, we have to be smart," he mutters. "No more risks. No more mistakes."

> "Agreed." Alara nods.
And just like that—
The moment they decide to protect Caleb is the moment their lives change forever.

The Mystery Man Returns to the Abandoned House

The night is darker now. The streetlights flicker faintly, casting eerie shadows over the abandoned house. The air is still, filled only with the sound of distant traffic.

A car slowly pulls up, its headlights off.

The mystery man steps out, his boots crunching against the gravel. His coat shifts with the wind as he looks up at the house—the last place he saw Caleb.

He was so close. But now, he's one step behind.

> "This is the place... the place where he was hidden."

His voice is low, measured. Not angry, not frustrated—just calculating.

He steps forward, pushing open the old wooden door with ease.

Inside the House – Searching for Clues

The house is exactly as he left it—but now, it's emptier. Caleb's presence is gone, yet the air still feels different.

He walks slowly, methodically. Examining. Studying. Looking for anything they might have left behind.

-The dust has been disturbed. Someone was definitely here recently.
-A faint imprint of a hand on an old table—Caleb's?
-The blanket Caleb used still lies in the corner.

He kneels, running his fingers over the fabric. It's still faintly warm.

> "Not long ago."

He straightens, his eyes flicking toward the doorframe. Scuff marks. Someone left in a hurry.

Then he notices something else.

A footprint in the dust.

> "A woman..." he murmurs.

His mind sharpens. Caleb wasn't alone. Someone took him—a woman, and at least one other person.

A New Lead – They Left a Trail

As he steps outside, he kneels near the ground. The faintest imprint of tire marks remains in the dirt.
After scanning the footprints, the tire marks, the disturbed dust, the mystery man knows enough.

He stands at the edge of the abandoned house, silent, calculating.

> "They think they've won."

A faint smirk flickers across his face.

They got him for now—but that won't last. They made a mistake.

They took him from the open into hiding.

But hiding always leads to patterns.
Patterns lead to weakness.
And weakness... is how you catch prey.

He pulls out his phone but doesn't make a call. Instead, he just watches the screen, his fingers hovering over a list of contacts.

> Not yet.

He slips the phone back into his pocket. He's in no rush. The best way to trap someone is to make them believe they're safe.
He turns back to the house one last time, eyes scanning the darkness as if listening to the air itself.
Then, without a sound—he disappears into the night.

The Mystery Man's Next Move

The mystery man sits alone in his car, parked in an empty lot. The glow of a laptop screen lights up his face as he watches the videos again.

The first video: grainy footage of Caleb doing something unnatural.

The second video: Caleb running, disappearing into the night.

> "Who are you?" he mutters under his breath.

He pauses the video at a close-up of Caleb's face. Young. Unassuming. But there's something else. Something that doesn't fit.

His fingers tap the keyboard. He's good at finding people. It's what he does.

He starts by tracking where the video was first recorded.

- One lead: The footage came from a youth home.
- If he was staying there... they might have records.

The mystery man leans back in his seat, a small smirk forming.

> "Alright, kid. Let's start there."

He shuts the laptop, starts the car, and drives into the night—heading straight for the youth home.

The Mystery Man Visits the Youth Home

The sun is high, casting long shadows over the worn-down youth home. Kids move in and out of the building, some playing, others watching as a black car pulls up across the street.

A man steps out. Calm. Unhurried. Purposeful.

He crosses the street, adjusting his sleeves, scanning his surroundings.

> "Nice place." His voice is smooth, neutral, as he steps inside.

Inside – Asking Questions

The inside of the youth home is busy. Staff move around, helping younger kids, while older ones linger in the hallways. The air smells like cheap coffee and old books.

The mystery man moves effortlessly through the space, blending in like he belongs.

At the front desk, a woman in her 50s, slightly distracted, looks up.

> "Can I help you, sir?"
He gives a polite, easy smile.

> "I was hoping to speak with someone who's been staying here."
> She frowns. "Are you a caseworker?"

> "No, just... looking for someone." His voice stays light, non-threatening. "A boy. He was here not too long ago. Dark hair. Quiet type."

She hesitates.

> "We don't give out information on the kids here."

He expected that.

He doesn't push. Instead, his eyes shift, catching sight of a small group of teenagers sitting near the staircase.
They're watching him. Curious. Suspicious.

Perfect.

The Kids Give Him a Clue

He steps away from the front desk, moving casually toward the teens.

They don't run. They just watch him.

> "You guys hear anything about a kid who used to stay here?" He speaks casually, like he's just making conversation. "Noticed him in a couple of videos online."

They exchange glances.

One of them—a boy, about 16, leans back against the railing.

> "You a cop?"

The mystery man chuckles, shaking his head.

> "Do I look like a cop?"

The kid smirks. "Nah, but you don't look like a friend either."

The mystery man tilts his head, amused.

> **"Smart."**

The other kids glance at each other, unsure if they should talk. But curiosity always wins.

> "The guy you're looking for... yeah, he was here." The teen shrugs. "Didn't talk much. Kept to himself."

> "He still here?"
The kid shakes his head.

> "Ran off a few days ago. Think he was scared of something."
That part interests him.

> **"Scared?"**

The teen hesitates. Then, leans in slightly.

> "Dunno, man. He wasn't like the rest of us. Something about him was just... different."
The mystery man watches him closely.

> "Different how?"
The kid shrugs, but something flickers in his eyes. Like he knows more but isn't saying.

The mystery man smirks, tossing a few bills on the railing.

> "If you remember anything else, let me know."

The kids don't touch the money right away. They just watch as he leaves.

Back in the Car – Piecing It Together

Sliding into the driver's seat, the mystery man leans back, thinking.

He ran away. But from what?

He was scared. Of who? Of what?

He drums his fingers against the steering wheel.

> "You're making this interesting, kid."

He glances in the rearview mirror—just for a second.

And that's when he sees it.

One of the kids—the same one who spoke—standing outside, watching him leave.

Almost like he regrets saying anything.

The mystery man just smiles to himself.

He starts the engine.

> "I'll see you soon, whoever you are."
And with that, he drives away—one step closer to finding Caleb.

Alara and Ethan Dig Deeper into the Text

Caleb is still in shock from his vision. The weight of the pyramids, the pharaohs, the mysterious child, and the words "My son... the one who will last for centuries" linger in his mind.

But right now, he doesn't want to talk.

So, while Caleb takes a moment alone, Alara and Dr. Ethan Carter retreat to the research area, determined to find out what the ancient text is really saying.

Inside the Research Lab

The research facility is quiet, filled with the hum of old projectors and glowing computer screens. A massive wooden table in the center holds stacks of aged manuscripts, crumbling texts, and scattered translation notes.

Ethan flips through his notes, eyes narrowed.

> "This text... it's unlike anything we've ever studied before."

Alara, standing nearby with arms crossed, watches as he zooms in on a digital scan of the manuscript. The translation is partially completed, but it's still full of gaps and cryptic phrases.

She leans in.

> "Do you think the vision Caleb saw is... connected to this?"

Ethan exhales sharply, adjusting his glasses.
> "Alara, at this point? I think everything is connected."

The Text Reveals a Hidden Meaning

Ethan pulls up the section they read earlier—the part that described:

- ✔ A lost bloodline
- ✔ A child hidden from time
- ✔ The coming of the serpent

But as Ethan cross-references different translations, he notices something they overlooked.

His expression shifts.

> "Wait a second…"

Alara leans closer. "What?"

> "This isn't just talking about a prophecy." He points at a specific line. "It's describing an actual event that already happened."

Alara's eyes widen. "You mean… in the past?"

Ethan nods.

> "A child. A royal child. Taken from his time, hidden away… waiting for the right moment to return."

Alara's Growing Suspicion

Alara's breath catches. She looks over at the manuscript, then at Caleb—still sitting across the room, lost in thought.

Her gut tells her something she's not ready to admit.

> "Ethan..." Her voice is quieter now. "What if this isn't just a myth?"
Ethan hesitates, but he can see it too. The text. The vision. Caleb's mark.

It's all too much to ignore.

> "If that's true..." Ethan swallows hard. "Then we're not just dealing with history anymore. We're dealing with something far bigger."

Caleb Overhears Alara & Ethan's Conversation

After the intense discussion about the ancient text, Alara and Ethan step away from Caleb, moving into the next room to talk privately.

They think they're alone.

They think Caleb is too distracted, too shaken by his vision to listen.

But they don't know what he can do.

Alara's Growing Worry

Alara crosses her arms, pacing the room.

> "Ethan... what if we're right?" Her voice is low, almost a whisper. "What if Caleb isn't just some lost kid? What if he really is... connected to all of this?"
Ethan sighs, rubbing his temple.

> "Alara, we need more proof. We can't just assume."

Alara turns to him sharply.

> "We found a text that talks about a lost child—a child taken out of time." She leans in, voice firm. "Caleb just had a vision about the past. And you want to wait for more proof?"

Ethan hesitates. He can't deny it.

> "...If this is real," he mutters, "then we have to protect him at any cost."
Alara nods, her expression serious.

> "Agreed."

Caleb Hears Everything

Across the hall, sitting alone, Caleb closes his eyes.

He doesn't need to move closer.
He doesn't need to strain.

Because his hearing sharpens, cutting through walls, picking up every word.

Their voices are as clear as if they were standing right in front of him.

His hands grip the armrests of his chair.

> "…A lost child."
"…Taken out of time."
"…If this is real… we have to protect him."
His heartbeat slows, his breath steady.

> They're talking about me.
For the first time, he realizes—he isn't just being studied. He isn't just a mystery to them.
> They're afraid of what this means.

Caleb Walks In at the Worst (or Best) Moment

Alara and Ethan are deep in their conversation, completely unaware that Caleb has been listening the entire time.

> "If this is real..." Ethan mutters. "Then we have to protect him at any cost."
Alara nods, her expression serious. "Agreed."

Then—

> "Protect me from what exactly?"

Both of them jump.

They spin around to see Caleb standing in the doorway, arms crossed, looking directly at them.

Alara's mouth opens slightly, caught off guard. Ethan just rubs his forehead, already exhausted.

> "How long have you been standing there?" Ethan asks.
Caleb shrugs. "Long enough."

Silence.

> "...You heard everything, didn't you?" Alara sighs, already knowing the answer.
> Caleb tilts his head. "It's not my fault you two talk so loud."
Ethan scoffs. "We were whispering."
> Caleb smirks. "Yeah, about that... turns out, I can hear things normal people can't."

Alara and Ethan exchange a look.

Oh. So now they have proof his abilities are real.

> "So." Caleb steps further into the room. "What was that about me being 'taken out of time'?"
> Alara clears her throat. "Uh. We were just discussing theories."

> Caleb raises an eyebrow. "Oh, theories? Cool, cool." He pauses, then deadpans, "So am I an alien, a ghost, or the reincarnation of someone really important?"

Ethan groans and rubs his face. "I don't get paid enough for this."
Caleb Confronts Them—And They Finally Tell Him the Truth

> "So, am I an alien, a ghost, or the reincarnation of someone really important?"

Ethan groans, rubbing his face. "You're making this difficult, kid."

Alara crosses her arms, looking at Caleb seriously.

> "We're still figuring it out, Caleb. But what we do know is... you're connected to something ancient."

Caleb's smirk fades slightly. He expected them to dodge the question. Instead, Alara is staring at him like he's a puzzle she's desperate to solve.

Ethan flips open his notebook, tapping the pages.

> "The text we found, the one that described a lost bloodline? It wasn't just a prophecy."
> Alara adds, "It was history."

Caleb frowns. "Meaning?"
Ethan sighs. "Meaning someone like you existed before. A long time ago. And whoever they were... they were powerful."

Silence.

Caleb lets the words sink in.
> "...Powerful how?"
> Alara hesitates. "We don't know yet."
> Ethan leans forward. "But we're going to find out."
Caleb shifts his weight, uncertain.

He wanted answers. But now that he's getting them, he feels like he's standing at the edge of something big. Something he might not be able to turn back from.

> "...So what now?" His voice is quieter.

Alara and Ethan exchange a glance.

> "Now," Alara says, "we start looking deeper. Into you. Into your past. And into what's coming."

Investigating What They Already Have

After their conversation, the tension settles slightly. Caleb now knows he's part of something ancient—but that doesn't mean he understands it yet.

Alara pulls back her chair and moves toward a large research table, filled with:
- Old manuscripts with Egyptian hieroglyphs
- Translation notes Ethan has been working on
- A few scanned images of an artifact they haven't fully deciphered

> "Okay," Alara says, scanning the mess of papers. "Let's work with what we've got."

> Ethan flips through some notes. "We've been focused on the prophecy, but there's more here. We need to start looking at everything—not just what we think is important."

Caleb watches them, arms crossed. He still feels out of place. But deep down, a part of him knows that whatever they find—it's going to be about him.

The First Discovery: A Hidden Symbol in the Text
As Ethan scrolls through the digital scans of the ancient manuscript, something catches his eye.

> **"...Wait."**

> Alara glances over. "What?"
Ethan zooms in on a faded section of the scroll, adjusting the contrast.
> "This symbol right here... I thought it was just damage to the text."

> Caleb steps closer. "And?"
> Ethan's voice drops. "It's not damage. It's a hidden marking."

Alara leans in. "A marking of what?"
Ethan pulls up another document, comparing symbols side by side.

> "...It's the same symbol that's on Caleb's foot."

Caleb's heartbeat slows.
> "Okay, that's not creepy at all."

Alara and Ethan exchange a look.

This means **whoever wrote this text—whoever left these words behind—**they knew Caleb would exist.

As Ethan scans the text, he finds something—but it's not complete.

> Ethan leans in. "There's something here... but it's faded."
> Alara frowns. "Can you make it out?"

> "Part of it," Ethan mutters, adjusting the contrast on the digital scan. "The symbol looks like Caleb's mark... but the rest of the passage is missing."
Caleb steps forward, arms crossed.

> "Great. So I have a creepy ancient mark, and we don't even know what it means?"

> Ethan exhales. "Not yet."

Alara leans back, thinking.

> "Maybe we're looking at this the wrong way."

> Caleb raises an eyebrow. "How else are we supposed to look at it?"

Alara shrugs. "What if we don't find the answers in the text? What if we need to look at... you?"

Caleb Processing Everything Alone

After Alara and Ethan's revelations, Caleb needed space.

The research facility was too loud—not in sound, but in thoughts, questions, and truths he wasn't ready for. So he walked down the hall, through a quiet corridor, and into a dimly lit room, away from the research and the overwhelming weight of it all.

He leans against a desk, staring at his hands.

> "A lost bloodline. A child hidden from time. And somehow, that's supposed to be me?"

He exhales sharply, running his fingers through his hair.

None of this makes sense.

He should feel something—relief, excitement, purpose.

But all he feels is pressure.

Doubt Creeps In

> "What if they're wrong?" Caleb mutters.

What if this is all one big mistake? What if Alara and Ethan want him to be something he's not?

> "I'm not a pharaoh. I'm not some lost king. I'm just..."

His voice trails off.

Because deep down, he knows that's not true.

Something inside him has always been different. The reflexes. The instincts. The way he sees things before they happen.

This isn't normal.

And now? He has proof that his past is tied to something bigger.

But does he want that?

The Mark on His Foot—A Faint Reaction

A strange tingling sensation moves through his foot.

At first, he thinks he imagined it. But then—a faint warmth spreads from the mark.

Caleb freezes.

He slowly pulls off his shoe, rolling up the leg of his jeans just enough to see it.

The mark on his foot looks the same... but for a second, just a second... it glows.

A soft, golden hue, barely there before it fades. His breath catches.> "Okay. That's new."

The Press Creates Suspicion Around Caleb's Disappearance

A week has passed since the accident.

The world saw Caleb survive a car crash that should have been fatal. The video of him walking away without a scratch played on the news for days.

But now?

There's nothing.

No hospital records.
No interviews.
No updates.

Caleb has vanished.

And the media is starting to notice.

News Broadcast – The Mystery of the Missing Teen

LIVE BROADCAST – CNN Headquarters

A serious-looking news anchor sits at the desk, adjusting her papers.

> "It has been seven days since the shocking accident in North Carolina—an event that left doctors and witnesses speechless."

The screen flashes to the footage of Caleb's accident—the mangled car, the firefighters running toward the wreckage, and then...

Caleb stepping out. Completely unharmed.

The footage pauses on Caleb's face.

> "This unidentified teenager was seen walking away from the crash—without a single injury."
> "And since that moment? He's disappeared."

The camera cuts back to the anchor.

> "No hospitals reported treating him."
"No family or friends have come forward."
"No sightings. No statements. No trace of him at all."
She leans in, voice lowering slightly.

> "So, who is this boy? And more importantly... why has he vanished?"

Speculation Grows – Theories Begin

Three pundits sit at a roundtable, discussing the footage.

● EXPERT #1 (Skeptic):

> "There's a logical explanation. Maybe he ran away out of fear."

● EXPERT #2 (Conspiracy Theorist):

> "Or maybe he was taken. Maybe the government already knows something we don't."

● EXPERT #3 (Medical Scientist):

> "What concerns me is the medical impossibility. If this boy really survived with no injuries, we need to study why."

The discussion heats up.

Some believe he's a government experiment.
Some believe he's a miracle.
Others believe he's a fraud.

But one thing is clear:
People are asking questions.
And Caleb's disappearance is only making them ask more.

Back at the Research Facility – Caleb Watches the News

Caleb sits in front of a small TV screen, arms crossed.

The room is dim, the only light coming from the screen.

Alara and Ethan stand behind him, watching in silence.

> "…Well, that's not good." Caleb mutters.

Ethan sighs. "They're already making theories."

Alara shakes her head. "And the longer you stay hidden, the worse it'll get."

Caleb looks down, jaw clenched.

He wanted time to process everything.

But it looks like the world isn't going to give it to him.

Caleb's Desperation—He Runs Into the Forest

The research facility feels smaller every second.

The news won't stop talking about him.
Alara and Ethan keep looking at him like he's something more.
The texts, the mark, the visions—it's all too much.

Caleb can't take it anymore.

He Leaves the Facility—Running Into the Forest

He pushes open the doors and walks into the cold air.
No one stops him.

Maybe they don't think he'll go far.

But he does.

He keeps walking.
Then running.

The trees grow thicker, darker. The further he goes, the more the world feels silent.

Caleb Alone in the Dark Forest

The wind howls through the trees. The branches creak under the weight of the night.

He finally stops, hands on his knees, catching his breath.

> "What am I doing?" He mutters. "Where do I even belong?"
For the first time, he feels completely lost.

And then—

BOOM.

A deafening sound rips through the forest.

The ground shakes.

A bright light explodes in the distance, illuminating the trees in golden flames.

Caleb's heart pounds. He snaps his head up.

> "What the hell was that?"

Without thinking—he runs toward it.

Flashback: The Priestess's Mission in the Time of Pharaohs

Before the portal appears in the forest...
We see Ancient Egypt.

A great temple. Torches burn along massive pillars. A group of high priests stand in a perfect circle.
And in the center... stands her.

The Priestess.

Her robes shimmer in the golden light. Her bracelets jingle softly as she clasps her hands together. She is nervous—but honored.

A deep voice echoes through the temple.
> "The time has come."

The Head Priest steps forward, holding a sacred staff. The other priests begin chanting.

The words are ancient, powerful. Their voices rise and fall in rhythm, the sound vibrating through the walls.

The air shifts. A strange hum fills the temple.

The ground cracks.

And then—

A swirling portal of golden energy erupts in front of them.

The Priestess gasps, stepping back.

The priests watch solemnly.

> "You have been chosen," the Head Priest says.
"To step through time. To protect him. To guide him."
The Priestess's breath shakes. She stares at the portal.

The future.
It is unknown. It is dangerous.
But this is her duty.
She looks at the Head Priest.

> "Will I ever return?" she asks.
His face is unreadable. "Only if the Gods allow it."
She swallows hard. Then, she straightens her back, lifting her chin.

> "I will go."

With one final breath—

She steps into the portal.

Back to the Forest—The Portal Opens

Caleb bursts through the trees, his heart racing.

What he sees stops him in his tracks.

A portal of golden fire twists and turns, crackling like a storm. The ground around it is scorched, as if touched by something divine.

And then—

A figure steps out.

Wrapped in flowing robes of gold and deep blue.
Bracelets shimmer against her arms.
Her hair is braided in a style that hasn't existed for thousands of years.

Her eyes widen as she looks around. The trees, the sky, the air—this is not Egypt.

> "...This does not look like my place."

The portal behind her closes with a final burst of light. The flames vanish.

And then—silence.

Caleb stares.

She turns to him. Their eyes meet.

For a long moment—no one moves.

Then she whispers the words that will change everything.

> "It is you."

The Priestess Arrives in the Forest

The Portal Erupts—Caleb Sees the Impossible

Caleb stares, frozen.

The portal of fire and light crackles, energy rippling in the air. The ground beneath it is charred, the trees glowing in the eerie golden reflection.

Then—she steps out.

A woman wrapped in royal Egyptian robes.
Her necklaces gleam under the light.
Her bracelets jingle softly as she moves.
Her braided hair falls over her shoulders, decorated with golden bands.

Her dark eyes scan her surroundings, confusion crossing her face.

She expected grand temples, stone walls, and the scorching sun of Egypt.

Instead, she sees towering trees, cold air, and a stunned young man staring at her.

She whispers something in ancient Egyptian.

> "Ḥeḥ? Nyu t̠ꜣ t̠ḥnw?"
(Where... is this land?)

The portal behind her suddenly implodes, vanishing with a burst of wind. The flames flicker out, leaving behind silence.

She sways slightly, her hand reaching for her head. The time-traveling ritual took everything from her.

Her breath grows unsteady. Her vision blurs.

And then—
She collapses.

Caleb's First Reaction – Helping the Unknown Woman

> "Oh, sh—!"

Caleb rushes forward, catching her before she hits the ground.

She's light but completely limp, her breathing shallow.

> "Hey! Are you okay?!"

No response.

Her skin is cool, her pulse faint but steady. Whoever she is, she's not dead—but she's clearly exhausted.

Caleb slowly lowers her to the ground, kneeling beside her.

> "Okay, so... what the hell is happening right now?"

She doesn't move.

Her robes, the golden jewelry, the ancient symbols embroidered into the fabric—everything about her screams something out of a history book.

He's seen weird things before—visions, strange marks, the texts about a lost child.
But this?
This is different.
This is real.

She Wakes Up—And Kneels Before Him

A few minutes pass. The forest remains silent, only the distant sound of the wind rustling through the trees.

Caleb leans back, running his hands through his hair.

> "What do I even do? Call Alara? Ethan?"

Before he can decide, she stirs.

Her eyelids flutter. Her fingers twitch.

Then—her eyes snap open.

She gasps sharply, sitting up so fast it startles Caleb.

She looks around wildly, taking in the strange forest, the cold air, the night sky.

Then—her gaze locks onto Caleb.

Her breath catches. Her hands begin trembling.

Caleb raises his hands cautiously.

> "Hey, hey, it's okay—just... tell me who you are."

She doesn't understand his words.

But she understands him.

Her eyes fill with emotion. Her body shakes. And before Caleb can react—

 She kneels.

Her head bows low, her hands pressed together in a sacred gesture.

> "Ḏd mdw… nsw." (Spoken words… Pharaoh.)

Caleb freezes.

> "Uh—what?"

Her voice is filled with reverence, with absolute certainty.

She whispers it again, louder.

> **"Pharaoh."**

Caleb's chest tightens.
He shakes his head, stepping back. "No, no, no. You've got the wrong guy."
But she only kneels deeper.

Her voice is stronger, unwavering.

> "Nesu-Bity." (King of Kings.)

Caleb's stomach drops.
This isn't just a hallucination.
This isn't just a theory.
This is real.

Caleb Tries to Communicate with the Priestess

The forest is eerily quiet. The air still carries the scent of burned wood and energy from the now-vanished portal.

Caleb stares at the kneeling woman.
The Priestess—dressed in golden robes, her eyes filled with reverence—is still looking up at him like he's a god.

But there's one huge problem.

> "...You don't understand a word I'm saying, do you?"

She blinks.
> "Nesu-Bity." (King of Kings.)
Caleb exhales sharply, running a hand through his hair.
> "Okay. Cool. This is great. You're from the past. You're calling me a Pharaoh. And I have no idea how to talk to you."
She tilts her head, studying him. His voice, his tone—she doesn't understand his words, but she recognizes his confusion.
Caleb gestures toward himself.

> **"Caleb."**
She furrows her brows slightly. Repeats carefully.
> "Kaa-leb?"
Caleb nods. "Yes! Caleb."
She seems to take a moment to absorb that information. Then, placing a hand over her heart, she responds:
> "Sa-nakht." (My name is Sanakht.)

The Language Barrier—Something Starts Changing

For a few minutes, they struggle to communicate. Caleb tries gesturing, pointing, using simple words. But she only responds in Old Egyptian.

Then—something shifts.

She watches him carefully, her expression thoughtful. Then, slowly, she closes her eyes and takes a deep breath.
A strange humming energy fills the air.
Caleb feels a sudden warmth in his chest. It's not painful, but it's noticeable.
> "What are you—"
Before he finishes, Sanakht suddenly speaks.
> "Y-you... understand...?"
Caleb's eyes widen.
> **"...Wait. What? You—"**
She frowns, struggling. The words sound broken, forced, like she's learning them in real time.
> "...s-speak strange... w-words."
Caleb blinks. "You're speaking English?"
She nods slowly, her face full of concentration.
> "Not... all. Some."
Her voice is shaky, like someone unlocking an ability they've never used before.
> "Time... gives me words."
Caleb stares. "Okay. That's... kind of insane."

Meanwhile: Alara & Ethan Are Searching for Caleb

Back at the research facility, Alara paces near the entrance.

> "We should've stopped him."

Ethan exhales. "I know."
> "He could be in danger."

> Ethan grabs a flashlight. "Then let's go find him."
They head into the forest, their flashlights cutting through the darkness.
Alara's mind races. Caleb was overwhelmed. He left because he couldn't handle everything at once.
But something feels off.

She has this deep gut feeling—like they're about to find something they aren't ready for.

 Alara & Ethan Find Caleb with the Priestess

After several minutes, they hear voices.

Alara freezes. "...Wait."

Ethan listens. "Is that... Caleb?"

They step forward cautiously.

Through the trees, they see him.

Standing in the glowing embers of a burned clearing, talking to—

Alara's breath catches.

> "What the hell..."

Ethan stares in disbelief.

Because Caleb is standing face-to-face with a woman dressed like she stepped out of Ancient Egypt.
A golden Priestess. Kneeling before him.
And then—the Priestess slowly turns and sees them.
For a long moment, no one speaks.

Then—

> "...They are yours?"

She looks at Caleb for confirmation.

Alara whispers, barely breathing:

> "...Caleb, what did you do?"

The Priestess Acknowledges Alara & Ethan—But Doesn't Fully Trust Them Yet

The forest is completely still.

Caleb stands between two worlds.
Behind him—Alara and Ethan, wide-eyed, their minds racing.
In front of him—Sanakht, the Priestess of the Pharaohs, watching them carefully.

The tension is thick, like the air itself is waiting for what happens next.

Sanakht slowly rises to her feet, her golden robes shimmering in the faint moonlight.

> "...They are yours?"

She looks at Caleb, waiting for confirmation.

> "Uh... kinda?" Caleb hesitates, rubbing the back of his head. "They're my... friends?"

Sanakht tilts her head, studying Alara & Ethan.

Alara steps forward, cautiously. "Who is she, Caleb?"
> "I... don't fully know." Caleb sighs. "She just appeared. Like, out of nowhere. Through a portal."
Ethan blinks. "...A portal?"

Sanakht watches their expressions closely. She doesn't fully understand their words yet, but she can see their reactions.

Their shock. Their caution. Their doubt.

She steps forward slightly, her eyes never leaving them.
Alara tenses instinctively.
Sanakht notices.

> "You... fear me."
Alara and Ethan exchange a look.

> "...Well, you kinda came out of a portal in full-on Ancient Egyptian royal robes," Ethan mutters. "So yeah. We're a little freaked out."
Sanakht doesn't react immediately. She studies them a moment longer, then:

> "...You are not his enemies."
She nods slightly.

> "But trust... must be earned."

Caleb watches her closely. "You don't trust them?"
She finally looks at him again. "They have not proven loyalty."

Alara scoffs slightly. "Okay, wow. Not every day I get told I have to 'prove loyalty' by an ancient time traveler."

Sanakht turns to her. She watches Alara carefully, and then—
She smiles.

> "...You have fire in your heart."
Alara hesitates. "...Is that a compliment?"
Sanakht tilts her head. "It is truth."

A Growing Alliance—But Uncertainty Remains

Sanakht turns to Caleb again.

> "If they are your allies... then we shall see their worth."
> "Whoa, hold on," Ethan raises a hand. "Worth? Worth for what?"
Sanakht pauses, then slowly places a hand over her chest.
> "To protect the Pharaoh."
The words send a chill through Caleb.

Alara crosses her arms. "Okay, we really need to talk about that 'Pharaoh' thing."

Caleb sighs. "Trust me. I'm still processing."

Sanakht watches their interaction curiously. There is something different about these people. Their mannerisms, their way of speaking. They are not like the royal guards, the priests, the advisors she once knew.

Yet, there is something about them that feels... right.
> "...Perhaps in time," she says finally, "trust will grow."
Alara softens slightly. "...Yeah. Maybe."

Caleb exhales. "Okay. So now what?"

Sanakht meets his gaze.

> "...Now, you learn who you are."

The Priestess Promises to Reveal the Truth—But First, A Test

The forest is still, but the tension is thick.
Alara and Ethan stand frozen, their minds racing.

A woman—not just any woman, but someone straight out of Ancient Egypt—just stepped through a portal of fire and time. And now?

She's talking to them.
Like it's completely normal.
Like she didn't just shatter reality in front of them.
> "...This isn't happening," Ethan mutters under his breath. "This is some kind of hallucination. Maybe I hit my head on a shelf back at the facility."

Alara slowly turns to him. "If you're hallucinating, then we're both hallucinating the exact same thing. Which means either we're losing our minds together, or—"

She gestures at Sanakht, still standing before them, completely composed, like she belongs here.
> "...or this is real," Caleb finishes for her.
Alara shudders. "Yeah. And I don't like that option."

Alara & Ethan Struggle to Process This

Ethan rubs his face, still staring at Sanakht like his brain refuses to accept what he's seeing.

> "...Okay, okay, let's just—" He takes a deep breath. "Let's break this down. We have a time-traveling Egyptian woman, who is calling Caleb a Pharaoh, and she just expects us to be totally fine with this?"

Sanakht tilts her head slightly, unbothered.

> "It is not expectation. It is reality."

Alara throws her hands in the air. "Oh, well, that just clears everything up, thanks."

> Ethan scoffs. "No offense, lady, but you shouldn't even be here. You're supposed to be—" He gestures vaguely. "Dead? Buried in some tomb somewhere?"

Sanakht raises an eyebrow. "I was chosen."
> Alara frowns. "Chosen by who?"
Sanakht looks at Caleb.
> "By the Gods."

Silence.

Ethan laughs—an exhausted, disbelieving laugh. "Okay, yeah. Sure. Why not? Let's just add divine intervention to the list."

Alara pinches the bridge of her nose. "I need a drink."
> "You have fire in your heart," Sanakht observes.

Alara throws her hands up again. "Lady, I just watched you walk out of a flaming hole in the universe. My heart is allowed to be on fire right now."

The Priestess Makes a Promise—But First, a Test

Sanakht watches them calmly. She expected this reaction.

They are of this time, of this world. They do not understand the weight of history.

But they will.

She turns back to Caleb.

> "You have many questions."
Caleb nods, still overwhelmed. "Yeah. A lot."

> She dips her head slightly. "I will give you answers."
Alara and Ethan snap their attention to her.

> "Wait—seriously?" Alara asks. "You'll actually tell us what's going on?"

Sanakht pauses.
> "But first... a test."

Silence.
> Caleb blinks. "...What kind of test?"
Sanakht takes a step forward, her robes flowing around her.

> "I must see with my own eyes. If they are worthy of standing beside you."

> Alara raises an eyebrow. "Worthy? Lady, I don't even know if I wanna be standing beside him right now."
> Sanakht smiles slightly. "Then you should have nothing to fear."

Ethan groans. "I hate this already."
The Test of Loyalty
The forest is still, the tension thick as Sanakht's eyes pierce through Alara and Ethan.

> "This test is not for strength."
"It is not for knowledge."
"It is for loyalty."

Alara exhales sharply. "Oh great, a test based on trust. We just met you, and you expect us to prove something?"
Sanakht doesn't waver.

> "You walk beside him. You claim to help him. But do you follow because of destiny... or desire?"
Ethan frowns. "What's that supposed to mean?"

Sanakht studies them. "Many will come to him. Some will seek to use him. Others will wish to control him."**
She looks directly at Alara and Ethan.

> "I must know... which one are you?"
Caleb shifts uncomfortably. "Sanakht, come on—"
> "You wish for answers." She cuts him off. "You will have them. But not before this is proven."

The Test Begins – A Choice Must Be Made

Sanakht takes a small, golden dagger from her robes and walks toward Caleb.

She places it in his hand.

> "There is no greater loyalty than sacrifice."

She steps back into the darkness of the trees.

The wind shifts. The air grows heavier.

The test has begun.

The Test: The Choice of True Intentions

A voice echoes through the trees, deep and ancient.

Sanakht speaks from the shadows.

> "If you stand beside him for your own gain… then you must leave now."
"If you remain, you must be willing to sacrifice something."
"There is no power without cost."

Then—the air grows colder.
A wall of shadows begins forming behind Alara and Ethan, closing them in.

They cannot leave.
They cannot run.
They must decide.

Sanakht's voice is calm, yet filled with power.

> "To prove your loyalty, you must take the dagger."

"You must each make an offering. A sacrifice."

Alara shakes her head. "Whoa, whoa—hold up. What kind of sacrifice?"

Sanakht steps forward again, her eyes glowing faintly.

> "Something that matters to you."

> "If you are here only for yourselves, the dagger will know."

"If you are here for him, it will take nothing from you."

Ethan and Alara exchange a nervous glance.

The Moment of Truth – Who Are They?

Alara grips the dagger.

> Her mind races. Does she really want to go this far? She barely knows Caleb. This isn't her fight.

Ethan watches.

> He thought this was just research. A discovery. But this? This feels like he's stepping into something much bigger than he's ready for.

Caleb watches them both.

> He knows this is insane. He doesn't want them to suffer for him.

But deep down... he needs to know.

Will they stay with him when the world turns against him? Or are they just here for the mystery?

Sanakht waits.

The dagger feels heavy in their hands.

If they are here for the wrong reasons, they will feel pain.

If they are here for Caleb, they will feel nothing.

This is the truth of their hearts.

> "Make your choice."

The Test of Loyalty—Proving Their Devotion to Caleb

Sanakht stands before them, her presence commanding, the ancient dagger resting in Alara's hand.

The forest hums with unseen energy. The air is thick, heavy, watching.
> "Make your choice."
Alara grits her teeth, gripping the dagger tightly.

> **"Fine."**

She presses the blade to her palm, expecting pain. Expecting some kind of magic to hurt her.
 Nothing happens.
No burn. No sting. Just cold metal against her skin.
Sanakht nods approvingly.
> "You do not seek power. You seek to protect."
Alara exhales, shoulders relaxing slightly. "Told you."

Now—Ethan.
He hesitates, staring at the dagger as if it might explode in his hands.

> "This is ridiculous," he mutters. "I don't need to prove anything."
Sanakht tilts her head. "Then leave."
The words strike him deeper than expected.
His jaw clenches. "I'm not leaving him."

 He grabs the dagger.
Just like Alara—no pain. No resistance.

Sanakht watches him for a long moment, then nods.
> "You stand with him. Even when the storm comes."
The dagger shimmers faintly, as if acknowledging the truth.
Then—the unseen force around them fades. The air becomes lighter.
Sanakht steps forward, looking at Caleb.

> "They are worthy."

Caleb exhales a breath he didn't realize he was holding.

> "Good. Because I wasn't about to do this alone."
Sanakht smiles slightly. "You will never be alone."
The Truth is Revealed—Caleb's Royal Bloodline

The forest is still, but the weight of what just happened lingers in the air.
Sanakht steps forward, her golden robes flowing softly, her eyes now fully focused on Caleb.

> "You have many questions. And now, I will give you truth."

Caleb crosses his arms, bracing himself. "Yeah. That would be nice."
Sanakht's gaze deepens.

> "You are not just any child, Caleb."
"You are the last of the Pharaohs."

Silence.

Ethan blinks. "I'm sorry—WHAT?"

Alara's mouth opens, then closes. "No, no, no. That's insane. That's—" She points at Caleb. "He's just some kid. Not—" She waves vaguely at Sanakht. "—that."

Sanakht remains calm.

> "He is not just some child."
"His blood is royal. His lineage is sacred."
Her voice softens slightly, filled with reverence.

> "He is of the House of Ramses."

 The name echoes in the air like a thunderclap.

Caleb's stomach drops. His breathing halts.
Alara and Ethan look at each other, wide-eyed.

> "Ramses," Ethan repeats, his historian brain kicking into overdrive. "As in Ramses II?
One of the greatest Pharaohs of Egypt? THAT Ramses?"

Sanakht nods.
> "The blood of Pharaohs still runs in his veins."

The Meaning Behind Caleb's Lineage

Caleb takes a step back.

> "No. That's crazy. That's not—"
His hand instinctively moves to his foot, where the mark of the serpent lies.

Sanakht notices. Her eyes soften.
> "You do not believe. But you have always known you were different."
She lifts her hand, gesturing toward him.

> "The serpent chose you because you are the last of the line. The last heir of the Pharaohs. The one it has watched over for centuries."

 The serpent—the ancient wisdom that guided Pharaohs—has been protecting Caleb all along.
Caleb's head spins.

> "I—I don't know what to do with this."

Sanakht steps closer.
> "You do not need to know now."
"That is why I was sent—to guide you, to protect you."

She was CHOSEN to watch over him—the last of the bloodline.

Alara & Ethan Struggle to Process the Truth

Alara rubs her temples. "So let me get this straight."

She gestures at Caleb. "You're telling me this guy—who eats microwave burritos and wears ripped jeans—is a literal Pharaoh?"

Sanakht's lips curve slightly in amusement.

> "He is not yet."

Ethan runs a hand down his face. "Okay, hold on. Even if this is true—what does that mean? Why does it matter now?"

Sanakht's expression turns serious.

> "Because the world is shifting."
"The past has awakened."
"And soon, others will come for him."

 A warning.
Caleb's chest tightens. "Others?"
Sanakht nods.
> "Not all who seek you will wish to follow you."
"Some will try to control you."
"Some will try to destroy you."
 The storm is coming.
And Caleb?   He's at the center of it.

Caleb's Vision—The Desert Calls Him

The revelation hits like a storm.

Caleb's heart pounds as he takes a few staggered steps back.

> "No. No, this isn't real. This can't be real."

Alara and Ethan call after him, but their voices are distant, muffled.
His chest tightens. He needs air. He needs space.
He turns and walks away.

Fast.

Then faster.
Before he knows it, he's running into the dark forest.

The Vision—A Message From the Past

Caleb slows to a stop, his hands gripping his head. His breathing is erratic.
> "I can't—" He stumbles forward, knees hitting the ground.
Then— the world shifts.

The cold night air vanishes.
The wind changes.
And suddenly—

He's standing in the middle of an endless desert.

The sun blazes above him, blinding and merciless.
The sand stretches endlessly, shimmering like gold.

And before him—towering like gods—stand the Great Pyramids.

Caleb's lungs tighten.

> "No way. This isn't real."

But it feels real. The heat, the sand whipping against his skin, the heavy air of something ancient watching him.

Then—

A deep, powerful voice echoes through the desert.

> "My son."

The sky trembles. The ground vibrates beneath his feet.

> "You are my blood."
Caleb spins around, searching. "Who—who's there?"
Then—he sees him.

A tall, imposing figure standing atop the dunes, draped in golden royal robes, the crown of a Pharaoh resting upon his head.

His face is strong, wise, and eerily familiar.
Caleb's breath catches. He knows who this is.

> "You were preserved to wake up at the right moment."
> "To rise again."
> "To bring peace to the world."

Caleb steps back, shaking his head. "No. No, this isn't—"
> "Your time has come."

The sky turns gold. The pyramids seem to pulse with power.

> "Be strong."
"Use your magic."
A sudden, overwhelming energy surges through Caleb's body.
He gasps sharply, clutching his chest. His veins feel like fire. The power—the weight of it—it's too much.
> "Stop! I don't want this!"
The vision collapses around him.   Darkness swallows the desert.

Back in the Forest—Sanakht Finds Caleb Crying

Caleb snaps awake.

He's back in the forest, collapsed on the ground. His whole body is trembling.

His cheeks are wet. He doesn't even realize he's crying.

Footsteps approach softly.
Sanakht kneels beside him.
She doesn't say anything at first.
She just watches. Understanding. Knowing.
> "It is overwhelming." Her voice is gentle.

Caleb shudders, wiping his face. "I don't want this."
Sanakht tilts her head.

> "It does not matter what you want."
"It is who you are."

Silence.

Caleb exhales shakily, his fingers gripping the dirt.
> "What if I can't do it?" His voice is barely a whisper.
Sanakht watches him, then—
She slowly places her hands over his.   > "Then I will guide you."

Returning to the Research Facility

The forest is quiet, except for the soft rustling of leaves and the faint sound of footsteps approaching.

Caleb is still kneeling, his hands pressed against the cold earth, his body trembling from the vision.

Sanakht sits beside him, her presence steady, calming. She watches him with understanding—she has seen this before.

Then—
> "There you are!"
Alara's voice cuts through the silence.
Caleb slowly lifts his head as Alara and Ethan rush into view, flashlights in hand.
Ethan's expression is a mix of frustration and relief.
> "Damn it, Caleb. You can't just run off like that!"
Alara stops a few feet away, breathing heavily, then notices Sanakht.
> "...And I see she followed you."
Sanakht slowly rises to her feet, watching Alara and Ethan carefully.
Ethan crosses his arms. "Alright, enough of this 'wandering into the woods for dramatic moments.' Everyone back to the facility. Now."
> Alara nods. "Agreed. We're standing in the middle of nowhere, Caleb looks like he just saw the apocalypse, and I'm freezing. So unless someone has a better plan—"
She points toward the facility. "We're going home."
Caleb doesn't argue. He feels exhausted, his mind still spinning.
Sanakht simply nods.
> "Then we shall return."   And with that, they make their way back.

Alara & Ethan Process Everything—And Decide Their Next Move

The research facility is silent, except for the distant hum of machines and the faint sound of the wind outside.

Alara and Ethan sit at the research table, across from each other, both deep in thought.

Sanakht is nearby, standing calmly by the window, watching the outside world as if it's foreign to her.

Caleb? He's somewhere else in the facility—probably trying to wrap his head around everything.

But right now?

Alara and Ethan need to decide what happens next.
The Conversation—What Do They Do Now?

Ethan leans forward, rubbing his face. "Alright. Let's break this down."

> "We have a kid who just found out he's descended from a freaking Pharaoh."
"A literal time-traveling Priestess who's sworn to protect him."
"And apparently, a mystical serpent has been watching over him his entire life."

He lets out a dry laugh. "Yeah. Totally normal week."
Alara shakes her head. "Ethan, focus."

Ethan exhales. "I am focusing. And what I'm seeing is a situation that's getting way bigger than us."

Alara taps her fingers against the table. "Then we need to decide—are we in or are we out?"
 Silence.

Sanakht turns slightly, listening.
Ethan raises an eyebrow. "Are you seriously considering leaving him?"

Alara exhales. "No. Of course not. But let's be real here. Caleb's life isn't normal anymore. And if we stay with him, ours won't be either."
She looks Ethan dead in the eyes.

> "So if we're staying, we better be ready for whatever's coming."
Ethan leans back, crossing his arms. "You think something's coming?"

Alara gestures toward Sanakht. "She said it herself. Caleb won't be left alone. Some people will follow him. Some will try to control him. Some will try to destroy him."

 That reality sinks in.

Ethan sighs. "Then we can't just sit here. We need to start preparing."

Deciding Their Next Move

Alara nods. "Agreed. But first, we need a plan. A real one."

Ethan taps the table. "Alright. We have three major problems right now:"

1 We don't know what Caleb is fully capable of.

2 We don't know who might be looking for him.

3 We don't know where this is leading.

Alara leans forward. "Then let's start with what we can control."

They decide their next steps:

Step One: Figure out Caleb's abilities.

If Caleb is more than human, they need to understand his strengths, weaknesses, and limits.

Sanakht might be able to help him train.

Step Two: Prepare for outside threats.

The world isn't searching for Caleb yet. But eventually, someone will.

They need to stay ahead of that moment.

Step Three: Uncover more of the past.

Caleb's lineage, the serpent, the prophecy—they still don't have the full picture.

If they're going to help Caleb, they need to understand what's coming.

 The Moment of Truth—Alara & Ethan's Choice

Alara leans back in her chair, exhaling.

> "So, are we doing this?"

Ethan smirks. "You already know we are."

Alara nods. "Then we better get ready."

They look toward Sanakht.

> "I think it's time we ask her exactly what Caleb is capable of."

 They've made their choice.

They're staying.
They're protecting Caleb.
And they're getting ready for whatever comes next.

Alara & Ethan Decide to Call for Reinforcements

The research facility is dimly lit, the air thick with tension.

Alara and Ethan sit across from each other at the table, both deep in thought. The weight of their decision settles in.

Caleb is somewhere else, still trying to process everything.

Sanakht stands nearby, silent, watching. She already knows what they're about to decide.
 If they're staying, they need help. A lot of help.
 The Conversation – "We Can't Do This Alone"
Ethan exhales, running a hand through his hair. "We're in over our heads."
Alara nods slowly. "Yeah. We are."

She looks toward the door where Caleb disappeared earlier.
> "But we can't leave him."
Ethan sighs. "I know."
A long silence follows.
Then Alara leans forward, her voice firm.
> "If we're doing this, we need help. A lot of help."
Ethan scoffs. "You got a list of people who know how to protect a lost Pharaoh and stop an ancient prophecy?"
Alara smirks slightly. "Actually... yeah."
Ethan raises an eyebrow. "...You're serious?"
Alara nods. "There are people out there who know things—people who won't think we're crazy."
She looks him in the eyes. "And we already know some of them."

The Team They Need

Alara grabs her phone and starts listing names.

1 The Protector: The Former U.S. Military Officer

A tactical expert, trained in survival, combat, and security.

Dishonorably discharged for refusing to follow corrupt orders.

Knows Ethan from the past—a guy he trusts with his life.
> Alara smirks. "If we need someone who knows how to keep Caleb alive, we need him."

Ethan nods slowly. "Yeah. He's got the skills. But he doesn't trust people easily."
Alara smirks. "Neither do we."

2 The Egyptologist: The Brilliant Historian

A renowned scholar of ancient Egypt.

Considered a genius but also a bit reckless.

Worked with Ethan before, but their relationship is… complicated.
> Ethan scoffs. "I don't know if she's going to help or punch me in the face."

Alara grins. "Probably both."
Ethan sighs. "Fine. She knows more about this history than anyone. We need her."

3 The Hacker: The Cybersecurity Expert Who Used to Work for the Government

Once a high-level intelligence operative, now off the grid.

Knows how to erase digital footprints, hack into government systems, and track movement.

Alara's personal contact—they have a history.

> Ethan raises an eyebrow. "You know a hacker?"
> Alara shrugs. "Let's just say... we did each other a favor a while back."

Ethan leans back. "That's not concerning at all."
Alara smirks. "She's the best at what she does. If anyone can keep Caleb hidden, it's her."

4 The Mystic: The Controversial Professor of Ancient Mysticism (Female)

A brilliant but outcast scholar, laughed at by mainstream academics.

Has spent her life studying forgotten magic and ancient supernatural forces.

Knows Alara and Ethan from years ago—they once called her "insane"... but now? They need her.
> Ethan groans. "Oh, she's going to LOVE this."
> Alara laughs. "Yeah. She warned us years ago that history was hiding something bigger."

> Ethan sighs. "And now we have to call her and say she was right."

The Decision Is Made

Alara locks eyes with Ethan.

> "We need all of them."

> "Agreed."

They have their team.

Now?

They just have to convince them to come.

Calling the Team—Reactions & the Moment of Arrival

The research facility is quiet, the air thick with anticipation.

Alara and Ethan sit in front of a laptop and burner phone, ready to make the calls.

Sanakht stands nearby, observing—but saying nothing. She already knows not everyone will be easy to convince.

This is the moment. They need a team.

The Calls—Mixed Reactions

1 The Former U.S. Military Officer (Uncertain)

Ethan dials. The line clicks.

> Deep, rough voice answers. "Ethan? Haven't heard from you in years. This better not be a favor."

Ethan exhales. "It's bigger than that. We need your help."

> A pause. Then—"Help with what?"

Ethan glances at Alara, then speaks carefully.
> "Protecting someone. It's complicated."
> "...Complicated doesn't pay."

Ethan smirks. "This isn't about money. It's about keeping the right person alive."

A long silence.
> "...I'll think about it."

Click. The call ends.

Ethan leans back. "Not a no."

Alara smirks. "But definitely not a yes."

2 The Brilliant Egyptologist (Excited!)

Alara dials next.
> The voice answers instantly. "If this is about Ethan, I'm still mad at him."

Ethan rolls his eyes. "Nice to hear your voice too."
> She scoffs. "If you two are calling me together, it means trouble. What is it?"

Alara leans forward.
> "You're going to want to hear this."

She gives a quick summary—ancient bloodline, lost Pharaoh, a Priestess from the past.

> A beat. Then—
> "You're messing with me."
> Alara grins. "Nope."
> The voice on the other end is silent for a second. Then—laughter.
> "You had me at 'Pharaoh.' I'm in."

[3] The Cybersecurity Expert (Hesitant but Curious)

Alara dials again.

> The voice answers casually. "Alara? If this is about erasing your existence again, I charge double now."

Alara smirks. "Not exactly. I need a different favor."
> "...Oh?"

> "We need to keep someone off the grid. For real. No traces. No government tracking. No one can find him."
A long pause.
> "...Alara, what are you getting me into?"
> Alara exhales. "Something big. Maybe the biggest thing ever."
> "...I don't like that answer."
Alara leans back. "You don't like it. But you're thinking about it."
> "...Damn it. Fine. I'll come. But if this is insane, I'm walking."

4 The Mystic Professor (Excited!)

Ethan dials the last number.

> A confident, amused voice answers. "Ethan Carter. Calling me? This must be important."

Ethan exhales. "You always said there were ancient forces we didn't understand."

> A smirk in her tone. "Mmm. I did."

> Ethan leans forward. "We found one."

Silence.

> "…Well, well."

> "…I hope you're ready for what comes next."

> "Does that mean you're in?"

> A low chuckle. "Ethan. There's no way I'm missing this."

The First Two Arrive, Then the Surprise!

Alara and Ethan stand outside the research facility, waiting.

They glance at the road. No sign of the others yet.
> Ethan crosses his arms. "Think they'll all come?"
> Alara shrugs. "Two for sure. Two are on the fence."

Ethan nods. "Then let's hope they don't change their minds."
Then—headlights appear in the distance.

A car pulls up.
The first two step out.

The Brilliant Egyptologist and The Mystic Professor.

The Egyptologist grins. "Oh, you two look nervous. This already fun?"

The Mystic Professor smirks. "Let's just say... this is where the real story begins."

Ethan rolls his eyes. "Let's go inside."

They turn to head in—when suddenly—

Two more figures step out from the shadows.

Alara and Ethan whirl around.

Standing just behind them, arms crossed, grinning—

The Former Military Officer & The Cybersecurity Expert.

> The Military Officer smirks. "You really thought I'd sit this one out?"

> The Hacker grins. "Put your magic to work, Alara."
They're all here.

The team is assembled.

And now?

 It begins.

The Team Enters the Facility—And Their Reactions Are Priceless

The facility doors slide open.

The team steps inside, eyes scanning the place, taking in the atmosphere.

It's not a government bunker, not a secret underground lair—just a highly advanced research facility. But still...

 It feels different. Mysterious.

The Egyptologist whistles, running a hand along the sleek walls. "Damn. Didn't expect you two to be running a sci-fi operation."

The Hacker cracks a grin. "You sure this isn't some hidden NSA facility? You guys keeping alien secrets too?"

Ethan rolls his eyes. "Welcome to the unknown."

The Former Military Officer remains silent, his sharp eyes analyzing every corner, already assessing security risks.

The Mystic Professor stops in the middle of the room, closing her eyes briefly, as if feeling the air around her.

 Something about this place... carries a weight.

> "This space has already witnessed something beyond us."
Alara raises an eyebrow. "What's that supposed to mean?"

The Mystic opens her eyes, giving Alara a knowing look.

> "You brought something ancient here, didn't you?"

 They keep walking deeper.

And then—they see him.

Caleb's Reaction—"Who Are These People?"

Caleb is already there, standing near the central table.

He was waiting.

But he wasn't expecting this.

His eyes widen as he watches four completely new people walk in—each with their own distinct presence.

For a moment, no one says anything.

Then—

> Caleb blinks. "...Who the hell are all these people?"

 Silence.

Alara clears her throat. "Caleb, meet your new best friends."

Caleb raises an eyebrow. "You got me bodyguards?"

> Ethan smirks. "We got you a survivalist, a hacker, a historian, and an actual witch."

> The Mystic Professor scoffs. "Not a witch, Carter. But I do know things."

The Egyptologist grins. "I prefer 'genius historian,' but sure, 'bodyguard' works too."

The Hacker shrugs. "Honestly? I'm just here for the chaos."

Caleb looks at Alara, completely overwhelmed. "Why are they here?"

The moment shifts.

Alara's expression turns serious.

She steps closer, looking directly at him.

> "Because we can't protect you alone."

Caleb feels the weight of those words.

Ethan nods. "You have no idea how big this is, Caleb. But it's bigger than all of us. If we don't get ahead of it—"

> The Military Officer cuts in. "—Then someone else will."

That hits differently.

Caleb stares at them. These aren't just random people.

They know things. They understand danger.

They're here because of him.

> "...Okay," Caleb mutters. "Okay. So what now?"
Alara opens her mouth to answer—

But then—

The Priestess enters the room.

The Team's Reaction to the Priestess—Disbelief, Shock, and Chaos

The moment Sanakht walks in, everything stops.

The air shifts. The energy in the room tightens.

Her golden robes shimmer under the lights.
Her ancient jewelry softly clinks as she moves.
Her eyes scan the room, her expression unreadable.

The team stares.

No one speaks.

Then—

> The Egyptologist bursts out laughing. "Oh, this is a joke, right? Some kind of reenactment? You brought a cosplay queen to play 'Ancient Priestess'?"

Sanakht's gaze sharpens.

> The Mystic Professor takes a step back. "...No. This is real."

Silence.

The Military Officer tenses, watching Sanakht carefully, like assessing a threat.

The Hacker just blinks. "...So, uh. What are we looking at?"

Alara exhales. "That's the part where it gets complicated."

Sanakht finally speaks, her voice smooth and calm.

> "I am Sanakht. Guardian of the Pharaoh's bloodline."

The room goes dead silent.

The Egyptologist stares. "Wait. Hold on. Hold on. Did she just say—"

Ethan nods. "Yeah. She did."
The Egyptologist laughs again, but it's nervous now. "You expect me to believe—"
Sanakht suddenly steps toward her.
She lifts a hand, her fingers tracing an ancient symbol in the air.
The lights flicker. The air hums.
The Egyptologist stops laughing.

The Mystic Professor's eyes widen. "...That's real magic."

The Military Officer glances at Alara and Ethan. "You two have so much explaining to do."

The Hacker looks back at the door. "I could still leave. I could totally still leave."

But none of them move.

Because despite their doubts, their shock, and their disbelief...
They all know one thing.
This is real.
And they are already part of it.

Official Names for the New Team Members

1 The Former U.S. Military Officer (Protector)

* **Name: Jack Calloway**
* Background: A former special forces operative, dishonorably discharged for refusing a corrupt order. A man of few words but deadly precision. He's skeptical of all this Pharaoh talk but knows danger when he sees it.

> "I don't need to believe in magic to know when someone's a target."

2 The Brilliant Egyptologist (Historian)

* **Name: Dr. Rebecca "Becca" Langford**
* Background: One of the leading experts in ancient Egyptian history. Brilliant, witty, and a little reckless. Used to work with Ethan—they had a falling out years ago. Thinks this is crazy but also too tempting to ignore.

> "You're telling me a real-life Pharaoh survived thousands of years in his bloodline and NO ONE knew? Yeah. I'm in."

3 The Cybersecurity Expert (Hacker)

* **Name: Nova Sinclair**
* Background: A former top-level intelligence hacker who erased herself from the system. Smart, sarcastic, and unpredictable. She and Alara have a history of working in the shadows. Doesn't like working with people but loves a challenge.

> "Ancient magic, secret bloodlines, and government conspiracies? Ugh. Fine, I'll stay. But I'm not wearing a stupid robe."

4 The Controversial Mystic Professor (Occult Specialist)

* **Name: Dr. Miriam Vazquez**
* Background: A professor of ancient mysticism, laughed out of academia for her theories on forbidden knowledge. Knows more than she lets on. Believes there are forces in the world older than recorded history.

> "I told you history was hiding something. And now? You're finally ready to listen."

Sanakht Tests the Team

The research facility's main chamber is silent.

Sanakht stands at the center, her golden robes flowing as she examines the newcomers.

Caleb, Alara, and Ethan watch from the side. They already know what's coming.

But the others?

They have no idea.

Jack Calloway (the soldier) stands with his arms crossed, analyzing the situation like a battlefield.
Dr. Becca Langford (the Egyptologist) watches with curiosity, still trying to decide if this is a joke.
Nova Sinclair (the hacker) looks completely unimpressed, arms folded, one eyebrow raised.
Dr. Miriam Vazquez (the mystic) stands calmly, as if she expected this moment her whole life.

Sanakht takes a step forward, eyes sharp.
> "If you stand with the Pharaoh, you must prove yourselves."
The temperature in the room seems to shift.
The team exchanges glances.
Jack scoffs. "Prove what, exactly?"
Sanakht's gaze locks onto him.
> **"Loyalty."**
The air grows heavier.
Ethan mutters under his breath. "Oh, this is gonna be fun."

The Test Begins – The Blade of Truth

Sanakht raises her hand.

A golden dagger appears in her palm—shimmering, glowing, like it carries ancient power.

Becca takes a step back. "Okay. Nope. Nope. Nope. We are NOT doing blood rituals."

Nova groans. "Great. Ancient magic. This is why I don't do in-person meetings."

Jack narrows his eyes at the blade. "I don't like surprises."

Sanakht ignores their reactions.

> "This blade does not cut flesh. It cuts lies."

Silence.

Sanakht moves toward them.

> "If you are here for selfish gain, if your heart holds deceit—this blade will reveal it."
"If you are truly here for him, you will feel nothing."
The tension in the room skyrockets.
Jack mutters to himself. "I swear to God, if this thing stings, I'm walking."

Becca raises a finger. "Wait, but what if we're here for the history? I mean, I'm invested in Caleb, sure, but also, this is the greatest archaeological—"
Sanakht steps toward her. "Hold the blade and see."
No turning back now.

One by One, They Take the Test
Dr. Becca Langford – The Egyptologist

She hesitates, then takes the dagger, expecting pain.

Nothing.

She blinks. "…Huh."

Sanakht nods. "You seek truth, but not for yourself. You may stay."

Becca smirks. "Well, at least something in my life makes sense."
Jack Calloway – The Soldier

Jack glares at the dagger, grabs it without hesitation.

Nothing.

Jack nods. "Figured."

Sanakht studies him.
> "You do not need to believe in fate to stand against what is coming."
Jack shrugs. "I believe in protecting people. That's enough."
Nova Sinclair – The Hacker
Nova stares at the blade. "Ugh, fine." She grabs it, rolls her eyes.
Nothing.
Nova smirks. "Told you I was clean."
Sanakht watches her carefully. "You hide behind humor, but your heart is steady."
Nova raises an eyebrow. "Yeah, yeah. I'm a softie. Moving on."

Dr. Miriam Vazquez – The Mystic

Miriam doesn't hesitate. She touches the blade gently—like she already understands.

Nothing.

Sanakht watches her closely.

> "You have always known the truth was waiting."

Miriam smiles. "I have."

The Test is Complete—Sanakht Accepts Them

Sanakht steps back, nodding.

> "You are worthy to stand beside the Pharaoh."

The room seems to release the tension.

Jack stretches. "Well, that was dramatic."

Becca shakes her head. "I still can't believe I just went through an ancient Egyptian loyalty test."

Nova smirks. "I mean... it could've been worse. We could've had to fight a mummy or something."

Ethan grins. "Don't jinx it."

Caleb's Reaction—Processing Everything

All eyes turn to Caleb.

He looks at this group of people who just went through a test FOR HIM.

People he doesn't even know well.

People who just proved their loyalty.

> "...I don't know what to say."
Sanakht places a hand on his shoulder.

> "Then say nothing. Just know you are not alone."

Silence.

Caleb nods slowly. "Alright... then let's figure out what happens next."

The Team Assembles—"We Came to Work"

The research facility now feels different.

It's no longer just Alara, Ethan, Caleb, and Sanakht.

Now, Jack, Becca, Nova, and Miriam are here.

And they're not here to sit around.

The Moment of Commitment

The team stands around the central table, the screens glowing with data, maps, and old Egyptian texts.

Jack leans against a wall, arms crossed.
Becca sits on the table, casually flipping through old notes.
Nova spins a pen between her fingers, already eyeing the tech setup.
Miriam stands quietly, watching everything with deep interest.

Then, Jack speaks first.

> "Look, I didn't come here to sit around."
"We came to work. So tell us—what's the plan?"

Silence.

Then—Alara and Ethan exchange a glance.

Alara nods. "Alright. Let's get to work."

She grabs the tablet, tapping the screen. A large display lights up on the wall, showing what they've gathered so far.

The Breakdown

Alara points at the screen.

> "Here's what we know."

◆ 1 Caleb's Bloodline & The Pharaoh Connection

Caleb is the last descendant of Ramses II.

The serpent has been watching over him for centuries.

Sanakht was sent through time to guide him.

◆ 2 Caleb's Powers Are Awakening

He has superhuman reflexes, agility, enhanced vision, and senses.

There's something deeper inside him—magic tied to the serpent.

They don't know the full extent yet.

◆ 3 The World Doesn't Know Yet—But It Will

Right now, no government or enemy is actively searching for Caleb.
But it's only a matter of time.
When they do come, Caleb has to be ready.

Assigning Their Roles

Alara looks at the group.

> "We need you to use your skills. Here's what we need from each of you."

♦ **Jack Calloway – Protection & Strategy**

> "Jack, your job is to keep Caleb alive."
"We need security measures, survival tactics, and a real plan for when the world comes knocking."

Jack nods. "Got it. First step—assess weak points. If this is our base, I need to know how to defend it."

♦ **Dr. Becca Langford – Egyptologist**

> "Becca, we need to understand what Caleb's connection to Ramses truly means."
"Any hidden texts, forgotten prophecies—we need to know what history has hidden."

Becca grins. "I love a good mystery. I'll start digging into untranslated records."

♦ **Nova Sinclair – Cybersecurity & Intel**

> "Nova, we need to stay off the radar."
"Can you wipe Caleb from any government databases, erase anything tying him to the accident?"

Nova smirks. "Sweetheart, I can make it so Caleb never existed if you want."

Ethan laughs. "Let's not go that far."

> "Miriam, Caleb's powers are waking up, but we don't know how they work."
"We need you to figure out what kind of magic he's carrying—and how to control it."

Miriam nods, her eyes glowing with curiosity. "That... I can do."

The Mission is Clear

Alara crosses her arms. "That's the plan. We prepare. We learn. We train Caleb. Before the world finds him."

Silence.

Then—

> Jack cracks his knuckles. "Then let's get started."
Becca grins. "Finally, a challenge worth my time."
Nova smirks. "Time to break some firewalls."
Miriam breathes in deeply. "The past has returned to the present. Let's not waste it."

The team is ready.

And now?

The real work begins.

Caleb's Training Begins—The Path to Power

The research facility's training room is dimly lit, the air thick with anticipation.

Caleb stands in the center, his arms crossed, watching Jack Calloway and Dr. Miriam Vazquez as they prepare for his first real training session.

Alara, Ethan, Becca, and Nova watch from the sidelines. Sanakht stands nearby, silent but observant.

This is the moment Caleb begins to understand his true potential.

Jack's Approach – "Forget Everything You Know"

Jack walks up to Caleb, eyes sharp, posture rigid.

> "First rule of survival—forget everything you think you know about fighting."

Caleb raises an eyebrow. "Uh, okay?"

Jack circles him like a predator, arms crossed.

> "Your abilities are useless if you don't know how to use them."

Jack stops and smirks.

> "So let's see if those fancy reflexes actually work."

Jack moves FAST.

Before Caleb can even react, Jack throws a punch straight at his face.

Caleb's instincts kick in—he dodges without thinking, twisting away at lightning speed!

Everyone stares.

Jack chuckles, impressed. "Good. Now do it again."

The training officially begins.

Training Breakdown – Jack's Methods

* Hand-to-Hand Combat – Caleb learns how to fight without relying only on speed.
* Survival Tactics – How to analyze threats & react before they happen.
* Weapon Training – Jack gives Caleb a wooden staff to test his balance & control.
* Endurance – Caleb pushes his body to the limit—his strength is more than human.

Jack doesn't go easy on him.

Caleb gets knocked down. A lot.

But every time—he gets back up.

Miriam's Approach – "You Are More Than a Fighter"

After an exhausting session with Jack, Caleb is drenched in sweat, breathing hard.

> "Okay," he groans. "I think I hate you now."

Jack laughs. "Good. That means you're learning."

But before Caleb can rest—

Miriam steps forward.

> "Your physical body is only half of your power, Caleb."
"Now, we awaken the other half."

The room shifts. The energy feels... different.

Miriam gestures for Caleb to stand in the center.

> "Close your eyes."

Caleb sighs. "Is this where I start floating or something?"

Miriam smirks. "Something like that."

Caleb closes his eyes.

Miriam whispers words in an ancient language.

The room grows cold.

The air hums with unseen energy.

Then—it happens.

Caleb feels something stir inside him. Something deep, ancient, powerful.

His chest tightens. His veins feel like they're pulsing with fire.

His body begins to glow faintly—golden symbols appearing on his skin.

The serpent inside him is waking up.

Caleb's First Mystical Breakthrough

Everyone watches in stunned silence.

The air crackles. The lights flicker.

Becca whispers. "Holy—"

Nova leans back. "Okay, yeah, I'm definitely recording this."

Then—Caleb's eyes SNAP OPEN.

They glow gold.

A sudden wave of energy EXPLODES outward!

The walls shake. Papers fly everywhere. The entire room trembles.

Everyone stumbles back—except Sanakht, who remains still.

> "He is waking up."

Caleb collapses.

His eyes return to normal, his breathing ragged.

Ethan rushes forward. "Caleb! Are you okay?!"

Caleb nods weakly, gripping his chest.
> "I... I saw something."

The Team's Reaction to Caleb's Power Awakening

The training room is silent.

Everyone stares at Caleb, who is still catching his breath on the floor.

The air is charged, the walls still faintly humming from the energy blast.

No one speaks.

Then—

Nova's Reaction – "Okay, What the Hell Was That?!"

Nova slowly lowers her phone, still recording.

> "Okay, someone needs to explain what the actual hell just happened."

She gestures wildly at Caleb. "Because I signed up for hacking—not Egyptian Jedi magic!"

No one answers immediately.

Nova turns to Jack. "Well? You're the tough guy. Say something."

Jack crosses his arms, face unreadable.

> "...That was unnatural."

His voice is quiet—but serious.

> "I've seen soldiers survive impossible situations. Seen men do things that shouldn't be possible."
"But this? This is something else."

He looks at Caleb, studying him like a puzzle that doesn't make sense.

 Becca's Reaction – "This Changes Everything"

Becca runs a hand through her hair, still staring at Caleb.

> "Alright, let's get this straight."

She gestures at Sanakht. "You already told us he's descended from Ramses."

> "We accepted that."

She points at Caleb. "But this? This is different."

> "This means the legends were true."

> "The pharaohs didn't just rule—they had power."

 That realization hits the room HARD.

She turns to Miriam. "And you? You knew this was coming, didn't you?"

Miriam's Reaction – "Yes. And It's Just the Beginning."

Miriam's eyes glimmer with something between fear and excitement.

> "I didn't know when or how—but I knew this would happen."

She looks at Sanakht.

> "He's waking up. Isn't he?"

Sanakht nods slowly.

> "The serpent's wisdom is flowing through him."

Silence.

Miriam exhales. "This isn't just a bloodline, then. It's power—real power."

Ethan's Reaction – "And That Means He's in Even More Danger"

Ethan leans against the wall, rubbing his forehead.
> "Okay. So, let's assume we believe all this."
He points at Caleb.
> "If his powers are waking up, that means it's only a matter of time before someone else notices."
That realization sinks in.
Jack nods. "Exactly. Becca closes her eyes. "And when they do,
they won't be coming to talk."

Caleb Finally Speaks – "I Saw Something."

Everyone turns back to Caleb.

He finally catches his breath, sitting up.

His hands tremble slightly—but not from fear.

From something else.

> "When it happened... I saw something."

Silence.

> "I was in the desert. The pyramids were around me."
"I heard a voice. It called me 'my son.'"
"It said my time has come."

The room gets even quieter.

Becca swallows hard. "Caleb... that sounds like a prophecy."

Miriam nods. "A direct connection to the past."

Nova groans, shaking her head. "Of course it did. Because why not make this even weirder?"

Sanakht Reveals the Truth About the Serpent's Power

The training room is still heavy with tension.

Caleb sits on the floor, still catching his breath after the surge of energy that shook the entire room.

The others stand around him—watching, processing, questioning.

Then—

 Sanakht steps forward.

Her golden robes move like flowing silk, her expression calm but unreadable.

> "It is time you understand what is inside you."

 Silence.

Everyone turns to her.

Caleb swallows hard. "You mean... the serpent?"

Sanakht nods.

> "Yes. But it is more than a symbol."

The Serpent's Truth—A Power Older Than Kings

Sanakht kneels beside Caleb, looking him directly in the eyes.

> "The serpent is not just inside you, Caleb."
"It has always been with you."

The room seems to grow quieter.

She continues, her voice steady.

> "Long before the pharaohs, before the temples, before the pyramids—there were those who wielded power beyond understanding."

> "The serpent is not a creature. It is not a curse. It is wisdom itself."

The air feels heavy. Everyone listens, transfixed.

> "Only the chosen ones could bond with it."
"It granted the pharaohs their power—their visions, their rule, their divine connection."

She places a hand over Caleb's chest.

> "And now, it has awakened in you."

Caleb's Reaction – "So I'm Possessed by a God?"

Caleb's chest tightens.

His mind spins. This isn't just about being a descendant.

He isn't just a human with a special bloodline.

This is something far greater.

> "Wait... so you're telling me I'm possessed by some ancient entity?"

Sanakht shakes her head.

> "No. You are not possessed."
"You are the vessel."

Silence.

Becca takes a step back. "That is... a lot."

Nova pinches the bridge of her nose. "Oh my god, this is getting crazier by the second."

Jack crosses his arms. "So this thing inside him... what does it actually do?"

The Powers of the Serpent

Sanakht slowly rises.

> "The serpent gives its vessel many gifts."

She raises a hand—and suddenly, the golden symbols on Caleb's foot flicker to life again.

Caleb gasps, feeling the energy surge through him.

Sanakht continues:

* Enhanced Senses – Seeing in the dark, hearing things from miles away.
* Superhuman Reflexes – Dodging before an attack even lands.
* Strength & Agility – His body adapting, moving faster, reacting without thinking.
* The Sight of the Pharaohs – Visions of the past, the present, and what is yet to come.
* The Power to Command – A presence so strong that kings and warriors once bowed before it.

The room is completely still.

> "But power does not come without price."

The Warning – "You Must Learn to Control It"

Sanakht's face darkens.

> "The serpent does not choose lightly."

> "If you do not learn to control it... it will control you."

A wave of cold air sweeps through the room.

Miriam exhales sharply. "That means if Caleb loses control—"

> Sanakht nods. "It could consume him."

That reality hits hard.

Caleb swallows. "So what happens if I let it take over?"

Sanakht's voice drops lower.

> "Then you will cease to be Caleb."

Silence.

Jack clenches his jaw. "Then we don't let that happen."

Nova's Discovery—"We Might Have a Problem"

Nova's fingers fly across the keyboard, cross-referencing searches, IP addresses, and underground networks.

Then, she freezes.

> "Oh, crap."

The room tenses.

Ethan leans in. "What?"

Nova tilts the screen, showing them the data.

> "I found someone."

A profile appears—a man asking about Caleb.

> "He's been poking around since the accident. He went to that house Caleb was hiding in."
"And now? He's got a team."

Silence.

Jack steps forward. "Is he a threat?"

Nova shrugs.

> "Right now? He's just digging. But if he finds something useful..."

Jack nods, already thinking ahead.

> "Then we make sure he doesn't."

The first real external problem has begun.

The Team Decides to Watch—Not Act... Yet

The room is tense.

Nova sits at her laptop, fingers still hovering over the keyboard. The screen glows with data—records of the mysterious man's searches, his movements, his growing interest in Caleb.

Jack leans against the wall, arms crossed, studying the information carefully.

Caleb stays quiet, watching them process the situation.

Then—Jack breaks the silence.

> "We don't move on him."

Everyone looks at him.

Ethan raises an eyebrow. "You sure?"

Jack nods.

> "If we go after him now, we risk making him more interested."
"We let him keep looking—but we make sure he doesn't find anything."

The strategy is set.

Nova Sets Up a Digital Shadow

Nova starts working fast, her fingers flying across the keyboard.

> "Alright, I'll keep an eye on him. If he gets too close, I can throw him off."

Ethan nods. "Can you make it seem like Caleb never existed?"

Nova grins.

> "Oh, sweetie, I can make it seem like Caleb was born on Mars."

The team smirks, but the tension remains.

Caleb's Reaction—Processing the Danger

Caleb leans against the table, arms crossed.

He's never had to think about people hunting him before.

Now?

> "So... what happens if he actually finds something?"

Jack looks at him, eyes sharp.

> "Then we deal with him."
The room goes silent.

Caleb Pushes Himself—Training Intensifies

The research facility's training room is quiet. Too quiet.

Caleb stands in the center, fists clenched. His heart pounds—not from exhaustion, but from something deeper.

He knows. Someone is looking for him.

The weight of that reality settles in.

He looks up at Jack, who watches him like a drill sergeant.

Miriam stands nearby, observing—not just Caleb's body, but his energy.

This isn't just training anymore. It's survival.

> **"Again."**

Jack's voice is sharp, commanding.

Caleb grits his teeth. He's tired. He's sore. But he doesn't stop.

He moves—faster than before.

Jack's Training – Caleb Learns to Fight Smart

Jack throws a punch—Caleb dodges.
Jack swings a kick—Caleb moves before it lands.

But Jack isn't letting him win.

He feints—then lands a blow to Caleb's ribs.

Caleb staggers back, gasping.

> "You're fast, but you're not thinking." Jack steps forward. "Your reflexes won't always save you. Use your mind."

Caleb nods, adjusting his stance.

> **"Again."**

They go at it again—Caleb dodging, striking, moving with purpose.

He's learning. He's adapting.

Miriam's Training – Awakening the Serpent's Power

Jack steps back, wiping sweat from his forehead. "Alright. That's enough from me."

Now, it's Miriam's turn.

She walks toward Caleb, her eyes glowing with curiosity.

> "You've improved physically. But your true power isn't in your body, Caleb."

She motions for him to sit.

> "Now... we test your connection to the serpent."

Caleb hesitates. He remembers the last time—when the power nearly exploded out of him.

> "I don't know if I can control it."

Miriam smiles. "That's why we practice."

Caleb sits. Closes his eyes. Breathes.

Miriam whispers in an ancient language.

The Energy Awakens—Caleb's Senses Expand

The mark on his foot burns slightly.

The energy moves through his body—powerful, but not wild.

Then—he feels it.

His hearing sharpens. He can hear the faint hum of wires in the walls.
His vision shifts. Even with his eyes closed, he can see the room in his mind.
The air around him hums. He senses the movement of everyone in the room.

Then—something new happens.

His body feels lighter. Stronger. Almost... weightless.

Miriam watches closely. "Good. You're not resisting it this time."

Caleb's First Vision—But It's Too Much

Miriam watches as Caleb relaxes into the energy, his senses heightening.

Then, she whispers something in ancient Egyptian.
> "See beyond."
Something clicks inside Caleb's mind.

His breathing slows. His body tingles. His foot—the mark—feels like it's pulsing.

Then—his world shifts.

Caleb's Vision—What Does He See?
He is no longer in the training room.
He stands in the desert.

The pyramids rise before him, towering under a blood-red sky.
The wind howls, filled with whispers.
Then—he hears a voice. Deep. Ancient. Calling to him.
> "My son... you must awaken..."
Caleb's heart pounds.

Suddenly—he sees figures in the distance. Soldiers? No... warriors. Ancient and modern, standing together. Preparing for battle.

Then—another flash. A golden throne. A crown. A serpent coiling around it.
And then—darkness.
Caleb snaps back to reality, gasping for air!

The Aftermath—The Team Reacts

Caleb falls forward, gripping the floor. His body is shaking.

 Everyone rushes toward him.

> Ethan grabs his shoulder. "Caleb! What the hell just happened?!"

Miriam kneels beside him, her face serious.

> "He saw something."

> Jack narrows his eyes. "What did you see?"

 Caleb looks up, breathless.

> "...A war. A throne. And someone—waiting for me."

 The tension is thick.

Becca exhales, shaking her head. "Okay. That's unsettling."

Nova leans back, muttering. "Yup. Totally normal. No big deal."

The Mysterious Guy Gets Closer to the Truth

Somewhere in the city—far from Caleb's training, far from the team's security—one man is still searching.

A black car pulls up outside a small, run-down internet café.

A man steps out. His coat is slightly worn, his face shadowed by the low glow of the streetlights.

This is the mysterious man. And he's finally found something.

Inside the Café – A Lead on Caleb?

He steps inside, the smell of cheap coffee and old electronics filling the air.
A hacker-for-hire sits at a back table, typing furiously.

The man drops a folder onto the table.

> "Tell me what you found."
The hacker glances up. Hesitates.
> "You're asking about that kid from the accident, right?"
The man nods.
The hacker exhales, tapping a few keys.
> "Well, here's the thing... I don't know who he is, but someone doesn't want anyone to find him."

The mysterious guy tenses.

> "What do you mean?"

The hacker leans forward.

> **"Every time I try to trace his name, his records, his history—someone's erasing them in real time."

He spins the laptop around—showing multiple failed search attempts.

Someone is actively covering Caleb's tracks.

The man grits his teeth.

> "Who's doing it?"

The hacker shrugs. "No idea. But whoever they are, they're good."

The mysterious man clenches his fists. He was right. This kid is important.

> "Then I need another way in."

The Mysterious Man Learns Caleb's Name

Night falls over the city.

The mysterious man's car pulls up outside the youth home again.

This time, he isn't leaving without something useful.

He steps out, scanning the entrance. The place looks the same—run-down, forgotten, ignored. But tonight? Tonight, it might give him exactly what he needs.

Inside the Youth Home – A Casual Conversation... or a Setup?

The man walks through the halls, his coat heavy on his shoulders.

A few kids are still awake, huddled in small groups, talking quietly.
He spots a boy—maybe 16—leaning against the wall, flipping a coin between his fingers.
The man approaches.

> "Hey, kid."
The boy glances up, unimpressed. "You a cop?"
The man chuckles. "Do I look like one?"
The boy shrugs. "I dunno. What do you want?"
The man doesn't waste time.
> "A while back, there was a kid here. Short, dark hair. Quiet type. Ran off after a bad accident."
"You know who I'm talking about?"
The boy tilts his head, thinking.

> "...Maybe."

The man pulls out a $20 bill.

The boy smirks, snatches it, and pockets it.

> "Yeah. His name was Caleb."

The man's expression doesn't change—but inside, everything clicks.

He finally has a name.

The Moment That Changes Everything

The boy leans back, flipping his coin again.

> "Dunno where he went, though. Dude just disappeared one night."

The man nods, pretending not to care.

> "That's alright. I'll find him."

He turns and walks away.

Gets into his car.

And now, for the first time—he has a real target.

The Mysterious Man Starts Digging for Caleb

The city is quiet, the streets empty.

The mysterious man drives through the night, gripping the wheel.

He finally has a name—Caleb. But that's not enough. He needs more.

His next move? Find anything that connects Caleb to his past.

Step 1: Checking Local Records

He parks at a small, 24-hour internet café.
Logs into a secure database.

Types: "Caleb + accident + youth home"

Nothing useful comes up.

He frowns.

He digs deeper. Medical reports? News articles? Missing persons cases?

Something's wrong.

There's almost no trace of Caleb.

It's like someone wiped his records clean.

Step 2: Looking for Witnesses

Frustrated, he changes tactics.

He drives back to the area near the accident site.
Finds a late-night diner nearby.
Sits at the counter, scanning the room.

> "Hey," he says to the waitress, casual. "You been working here long?"

She shrugs. "Few years. Why?"

He slides a $50 bill across the counter.

> "Few weeks back, there was an accident near here. A kid—dark hair, kinda quiet. You see anything?"

She hesitates. But money talks.

She sighs. "Yeah... I remember him."

 His heart pounds. He's getting closer.

> "What do you remember?"

She leans in slightly, lowering her voice.
> "That kid? He should've died in that crash. But I swear, by the time the paramedics got there, he barely had a scratch."
 The man stays quiet, absorbing the information.
> **"Then?"**
She shrugs. "Cops took him to the hospital. After that? Gone. Vanished."
 Bingo.

Nova Discovers Someone is Searching for Caleb

Inside the research facility, Nova leans back in her chair, stretching. She's been monitoring Caleb's digital footprint for hours—so far, nothing unusual.

Then—her screen blinks.

A new alert.

Her eyes narrow as she sits up, typing quickly.

SOMEONE is searching for Caleb's accident records.

Not just once. Multiple times. Across different platforms.

Nova Reacts – "Oh, Hell No."

> "Oh, hell no."

She types furiously, pulling up more data.

> "Who the hell are you?" she mutters.

She backtracks the searches, trying to pinpoint the source.

But whoever it is—they're good. They're covering their tracks, bouncing signals off different locations.

But Nova is better.

She smirks, cracking her knuckles. "Alright, mystery stalker. Let's dance."

She Traces the Searcher's Activity

She follows the trail—redirects IPs—cross-references timestamps.

Then she gets a hit.

It's coming from a public terminal. Some random café.

> "Smart move, jackass," she mutters. "But not smart enough."

She digs deeper.

The same user searched for Caleb's accident... and the youth home.

Then the abandoned house where Caleb hid.

Now? They're looking at hospital records.

Whoever this is—they're getting closer.

Nova Sounds the Alarm

She slams her hand on the desk.

> "GUYS! We've got a problem."F Within seconds, Alara, Ethan, Jack, and Becca rush into the room.

Jack crosses his arms. "Talk to me."

Nova spins her laptop around, showing the data.

> "Someone's looking for Caleb. Not just casually—they're putting the pieces together."

Silence.

Ethan leans in. "Who is it?"

Nova grits her teeth. "No idea. But if they keep digging? It won't take long before they figure out too much."

Jack Takes Action—The Hunt Begins

The research facility is no longer calm.

Nova's warning hit hard. Someone is actively piecing together Caleb's trail.

Jack isn't the type to wait around.

He pushes away from the desk, cracking his knuckles.

> "We can't just sit here while someone hunts Caleb. We need to find this guy—before he finds us."
 Everyone looks at him. The room tenses.

Ethan nods, serious. "Agreed. But how?"

Nova spins her chair, already working.

> "I've got a location—some internet café. If we move now, we might catch him before he disappears."

Jack smirks.

> "Good. Then let's pay him a visit."

The Chase Begins—Jack & Ethan Move Out

Jack and Ethan gear up. No weapons—just enough to intimidate if needed.

Time is ticking. Whoever this guy is, he's close to the truth.

The car speeds toward the café, tension thick in the air.

> Jack grips the wheel. "We go in fast. We corner him before he knows what's happening."

Ethan nods. "And if he fights back?"

Jack smirks. "Then he picked the wrong fight."

The mission is clear—stop him before he finds Caleb.

At the Café—The Target Is There

They pull up fast. No hesitation.

The café is dimly lit, a few late-night customers inside.

And then—they see him.

The mysterious man, sitting at a computer, still searching.

Jack and Ethan exchange a look. It's now or never.

They move. Fast.

They enter the café, splitting up—one on each side, boxing him in.

The man doesn't notice yet. He's too focused on his screen.

Jack steps up behind him.

Slams a hand down on the table.

> "Hey, buddy. You look busy."

The man stiffens. He knows something is wrong.

He glances up, eyes meeting Jack's. Then Ethan's.

He realizes—he's trapped.

The tension explodes.

> Jack leans down, voice low. "You're gonna tell me exactly what you know. Right now."

The Interrogation—A Shocking Truth

The café is dead silent.
Jack leans in close, voice sharp.
> "You're gonna tell me exactly what you know. Right now."
The mysterious man swallows, glancing at Ethan, then back at Jack.

He knows he's outmatched.
But then... he smirks.
Jack narrows his eyes. "Something funny?"

The man tilts his head.
> "You think I'm the only one looking for him?"

Silence. That single sentence changes everything.

Jack grabs him by the collar. "What did you just say?"

The man doesn't resist. He leans in instead.

> "I'm not your problem. The people coming next? They are."

Jack & Ethan Exchange a Look—This Just Got Worse

Ethan tenses. "Who's coming?"

The man just smiles.

> "You'll see soon enough."

Jack's grip tightens. "Tell me."

> "Or what? You'll take me out?"
"Go ahead. It won't change what's coming."

The tension is thick.

Jack knows this guy isn't bluffing.

Someone else is already looking for Caleb. Someone bigger.

A "Gentle" Interrogation—Jack's Way

The café is dead silent.

The mysterious man smirks, but his confidence is cracking.

Jack leans in closer, gripping the table.

> "You just said we're not your biggest problem."
"That means you know something we don't."

Jack grabs the guy by the collar—just enough to make his point.

Ethan stands behind him, arms crossed—silent, but dangerous.

The man exhales, trying to keep his cool.
> "You really wanna know?" He chuckles. "Then listen close."
He leans forward. His voice drops to a whisper.
> "You're already too late."
Jack doesn't react—but internally? That's NOT what he wanted to hear.

Ethan's Turn—No More Games

Ethan steps in, voice sharp.

> "Too late for what?"

The man just smiles.

Ethan slams his fist on the table—loud enough to make the whole café jump.

> "Enough games. Talk."

The guy finally sighs.

> "Alright, alright. You really wanna know?"

He looks Jack dead in the eye.

> "Caleb's name isn't just floating around randomly."
"There are people—real powerful people—who are interested in him."

Jack and Ethan exchange a glance.

> **"Who?"**

The man smirks.

> "That's the fun part, isn't it? Figuring it out before they find you first."

Tension hangs heavy in the air.

Jack Puts Him to Sleep- The Hard Way

The air in the café is thick with tension. Jack exhales slowly, flexing his fingers. Ethan watches the man closely, waiting for the next move. But Jack's already decided. "You talk too much." Before the man can react- Jack delivers a clean, precise punch to his jaw. The man's head jerks back-his body goes limp. He slumps forward onto the table- completely out. Silence.

Ethan's Reaction - "Was That Necessary?"

Ethan raises an eyebrow. "Was that really necessary?" Jack shrugs. "It was faster than listening to his cryptic nonsense." He checks the guy's pulse-still alive, just out cold.

Searching His Pockets—A Shocking Discovery

The café is still quiet, the mysterious man slumped over the table—out cold.

Jack rolls his shoulders, looking down at him.

Ethan crosses his arms. "We gonna just leave him here?"

Jack smirks. "Not before we see what he's hiding."

The Search—What's in His Pockets?

Jack quickly pats him down, checking for anything useful.

A burner phone – Locked, no fingerprints.
A folded note – Coordinates? A location? Strange numbers.
A small emblem – It's ancient-looking, Egyptian symbols on it.

Jack holds up the emblem.

> "What the hell is this?"

Ethan leans in, eyes narrowing.

> "That's not just some random trinket. That's... old."

This just got interesting.

Taking a Picture—Tracking Him Later

Ethan pulls out his phone. "Might as well get a photo—Nova will want to track him."

He snaps a clear shot of the guy's face.

Now, they have something solid.

Returning to the Facility—The Team Analyzes the Clues

The car speeds through the night.

Jack drives, his jaw clenched.
Ethan flips the small emblem between his fingers, studying it in the dim light.
They've got clues. Now they need answers.
Inside the facility, Nova, Alara, and the rest of the team are already waiting.

The Debrief—Laying Out the Evidence

Nova sits at her desk, scanning the burner phone.

Sanakht stands near the table, eyes locked onto the emblem.

The room is quiet—everyone focused.

Jack tosses the note onto the table. "Coordinates. No idea where."

Ethan places the emblem down. "And this. Looks ancient."

Sanakht's eyes widen slightly.

> "I know what this is."
Everyone looks at her.
The Reveal—The Emblem's Meaning

Sanakht picks up the emblem carefully, turning it over in her hands.
> "This... is a seal."
Silence.
> "It belongs to a forgotten order—one that has protected ancient secrets for centuries."
> "If this man had it, then he was not just a seeker of truth. He was part of something much larger."
Everyone exchanges looks.
Jack crosses his arms. "So we just punched out a guy from a secret society?"
Sanakht nods. "And now... they will come looking."
Tension fills the room.

A Night of Questions—Sanakht Opens Up

The facility feels quieter tonight.

For the first time since she arrived, Sanakht is not performing a ritual or warning them about the future.

She sits cross-legged on the floor, calm, reflecting.

The group—Alara, Ethan, Nova, Becca, Jack, and Caleb—watch her in curiosity.

It's Ethan who speaks first.

> "Sanakht... I have to ask. What was your life like? Before all this?"

Sanakht looks up, surprised. No one has ever asked her that before.

Sanakht's Past—A Glimpse into Ancient Egypt

She exhales slowly, her voice soft.

> "I was not born a priestess. I was chosen."

The room leans in—everyone wants to hear more.

> "I was raised in the great city of Waset—you call it Thebes. My father was a temple scribe, my mother a healer. We lived near the Nile, where the gods blessed our people."

Caleb listens closely. He's never heard someone speak of ancient Egypt like this—as if she was still there.

Becca tilts her head. "So, you had a normal life before all this?"

Sanakht nods.

> "I had brothers. Friends. We played by the river. We laughed. We lived under the eye of the gods."

A shadow crosses her face.

> "Then... I was chosen."

Becoming a Priestess—Her Sacrifice

Alara leans forward. "What do you mean, 'chosen'?"

Sanakht hesitates, then finally speaks.

> "The High Priest of Amun came to our home when I was ten."
"He told my father that the gods had spoken. That I had been given a gift—the ability to feel the divine presence."
"From that moment on, I was no longer just a girl. I was to be trained in the temples. I was to serve the gods, speak their words, perform their rituals."

Silence.

Jack frowns. "So... you didn't have a choice?"

Sanakht lowers her gaze. "No."

The weight of her words lingers.

Nova mutters. "That's kinda messed up."

Caleb finally speaks. "Did you ever want something else?"

Sanakht smiles sadly.

> "Perhaps. But fate does not ask what we want. It only reveals what we are meant to become."

A heavy silence. Her words feel... familiar. Almost like they could be about Caleb too.

A Story from the Temple—A Magical Tale of Ancient Egypt

The room is silent. The team listens intently, drawn into Sanakht's words.

Alara leans forward. "Tell us more. Something... magical. Something no one else would know."

Sanakht closes her eyes for a moment, as if pulling a memory from a distant time. When she speaks again, her voice is softer, almost reverent.

> "There was a night... a sacred night... when I first understood the power of the gods."

Everyone listens, completely captivated.

The Festival of the Living Gods

Sanakht looks at Caleb. "You would have seen it, had you been born in your true time."

She begins to paint a picture with her words.

Ancient Egypt, thousands of years ago. The temple of Amun-Ra stood tall and golden, its walls covered in sacred carvings.

Torches lit the great hall, where the priests and priestesses gathered for the Festival of the Living Gods.

A colossal statue of Amun-Ra stood at the center, its golden eyes staring down at them.

And then—the magic began.

When the Gods Walked Among Them

Sanakht's voice grows intense.

> "On the festival night, the High Priest called upon Amun-Ra himself. He recited the ancient words, the air in the temple grew heavy, and then…"

She pauses, looking at the group.

> "…the statue opened its eyes."

Silence.

Becca blinks. "Wait. What?"

Sanakht nods.

> "The god awakened."

She describes how the priests and priestesses fell to their knees, overcome with divine presence.

The golden statue turned its head. The torches flickered, casting shadows that danced like spirits.

A deep voice—one not of this world—spoke through the temple.

> "I see you, my children. And I bless you."

The entire temple trembled.

For one night, the gods were truly among them.

The Proof of the Divine

Ethan shifts in his seat. "You're saying... this actually happened?"

Sanakht nods.

> "I was there. I felt the power. I saw the gold of the statue glow with life."

Jack leans back. "Okay, so... if that's true, what happened after? Did the gods just... leave?"

Sanakht's face darkens.

> "The power faded with the rising sun. The statue's eyes closed. The voice became silence."

Nova smirks. "Sounds like a good show."
Sanakht looks at her, unfazed. "It was no show. It was the will of the gods."
Caleb listens, deep in thought. He isn't sure what to believe—but something inside him stirs.

Caleb Tells Sanakht About His Dream

The room is quiet. The group has been listening to Sanakht's story about Egypt.

But Caleb's mind is spinning. He remembers... the dream.

He's seen Egypt before. Not in books. Not in pictures.
As a child, he was THERE.
The pharaohs called him their son. They told him he would be preserved.

And now... he knows why.

He looks at Sanakht.

> "I need to tell you something."

Sanakht tilts her head. "What is it, my Pharaoh?"

Caleb hesitates—then finally speaks.

> "I saw it. Egypt. A long time ago. I saw the temples, the pyramids. But it wasn't a dream... it was like I was there."

Sanakht's face changes. She wasn't expecting this.
> "You... remember?"

The tension in the room thickens. Everyone is watching.

Caleb nods.

> "They told me I was meant to wake up in this time. That I was... preserved."

Sanakht stands up abruptly, her eyes wide with shock.

> "This is not possible…"

Silence.

And then… she drops to her knees.

Everyone stares. Jack, Ethan, Alara—none of them understand what just happened.

But Sanakht does.

She wasn't just sent to protect a descendant. She was sent to serve a lost king.

Sanakht Unravels the Truth

The air in the facility is heavy—thick with something unspoken.

Sanakht is still kneeling, eyes locked on Caleb, as if seeing him for the first time.

Caleb just revealed that he was not just a descendant—but that he was there, in ancient Egypt.
He saw the pharaohs, the temples, and the prophecy of his return.
Now, the priestess must face a truth she was never prepared for.
She finally whispers.
> "It was not just the bloodline that was preserved… it was you."
The others look at each other, confused. But Caleb is frozen, waiting.

Sanakht Explains the Impossible—The Ritual of Preservation

She slowly rises to her feet, her hands trembling.

> "There were rumors. Secrets passed down among the High Priests. That the gods had chosen one among the royal bloodline... one who would not perish, but instead be preserved beyond time."

She walks toward Caleb, eyes intense.

> "But this was no myth. It was YOU."

Caleb's pulse pounds.

Alara speaks up, confused. "But how? That's impossible."

Sanakht shakes her head.
> "Not to the gods. And not to the Order."
Jack frowns. "The Order?"
Sanakht exhales.
> "There was a sacred ritual—one that could preserve the body and the soul. But it was forbidden. It required an ancient power, one the pharaohs feared to use."
She turns back to Caleb.
"And yet, they used it—to save YOU." **Silence.**

How Did Caleb Survive Thousands of Years?

Ethan rubs his temples. "So you're saying... Caleb was frozen in time? Like, what? In a tomb somewhere?"

Sanakht's voice lowers.

> "Not a tomb. A sanctuary. A hidden place where only the priests of the serpent could enter. The Ritual of Preservation was unlike any other... it did not simply keep a man alive. It kept him untouched by time itself."

Nova's fingers tap on her laptop nervously. "So he wasn't asleep? He just... didn't exist in time?"

Sanakht nods.

"Until the world was ready."

Caleb swallows hard. He doesn't know whether to believe this or run from it.

Then he asks the question that's been burning in his mind.

> "Who did this to me?"

Sanakht meets his gaze.

"Your father."
The room explodes in silence.

The Truth—But Not All of It Yet

The facility is silent. Sanakht's words still hang in the air.

"Your father did this."

Caleb feels his stomach tighten. He doesn't know whether to believe it, deny it, or run from it.

Jack, Ethan, and the others exchange glances—this is beyond anything they expected.

Caleb finally speaks, his voice sharp.

> "Who was he?"

Sanakht exhales deeply, looking almost... conflicted.

> "He was a great Pharaoh. One of the most powerful rulers of Kemet."

Alara steps forward, her arms crossed. "That's not an answer. Which pharaoh?"

Sanakht's eyes darken.

> "You are not ready to know."

Silence.

Caleb clenches his fists. "You can't just drop this on me and expect me to accept it."

Ethan mutters. "She's protecting him. Whatever this is, she thinks he's not ready."

Jack frowns. "Not ready? He's already living it."

Sanakht remains firm.

> "There are truths that, if revealed too soon, will shake the foundations of your mind. You must first embrace what you are before you learn who you were."

Becca exhales. "Damn. That sounds dramatic."

Caleb shakes his head, pacing.

> "So I was taken from my time, frozen, or whatever, and now I wake up thousands of years later with no memories of my life? And you expect me to just... wait?"

Sanakht steps toward him.

> "You must. Because when you learn his name, you will not just carry his legacy—you will carry his burden."

The weight of her words is crushing.   Caleb breathes hard, his mind spinning.

Miriam Speaks—The Scholar's Perspective

Miriam steps forward. She hasn't spoken yet, but her mind has been racing.

As a historian, she's studied pharaohs, lineages, and myths—but THIS? This changes everything.

She looks at Sanakht, then at Caleb.

> "If what you're saying is true... then history is wrong. Everything we thought we knew about ancient Egypt—about its rulers, its beliefs, its power—it's all incomplete."

She turns to Caleb.

> "You are not just a lost pharaoh. You are living proof that the ancients knew something we don't. That they had knowledge, rituals, and power that we can't even begin to understand."

Nova mutters. "So, what? Caleb is walking history?"

Miriam shakes her head.
> "No. He is the missing chapter."
The room is stunned.
Caleb looks at Miriam, her words cutting deeper than even Sanakht's.
He is not just a mystery.
He is a secret that was never meant to be uncovered.

This is just the beginning...

The journey is far from over. Stay tuned for Book 2, where the mysteries deepen, the stakes rise, and Caleb's destiny unfolds like never before.

Coming Soon.